GW01459396

Solstice

Chris Elphick

"It's bedlam out there tonight," Dr Novak announced as he stepped into the staff room of St. Mary's Hospital. Stepping over to the coffee machine, he pressed the espresso button and waited eagerly for the polystyrene cup to fill with the black liquid. "It' times like this I wish they would serve something stronger in those god-damned machines."

"I heard the police have been called in to talk with the two latest patients on the ward." Staff Nurse Riley answered.

Dr Novak nodded. "Yes, that's why I nipped in here to grab a quick coffee before the Detective Inspector arrives. I don't think I will get another opportunity for a break after I speak to her."

"What's the story with the two patients?" Nurse Adams asked. I heard the girl has had a bad reaction to drugs and is suffering from some sort of psychosis."

"Kids, eh!" Dr Novak shrugged.

"The poor girl they brought in seemed delirious." Staff Nurse Riley added. "She was blubbering about gnomes and the supernatural. She was in a right state. The young boy they brought in with her though... There was something very off with him. He seemed almost malevolent."

"Did you see his eyes?" Nurse Adams chipped in. "It was like the devil himself was looking out at you behind those eyes."

Dr Novak ushered silence with an authoritative wave of his hand. "That lad has had more to worry about than strange-looking eyes." He said.

"Yes, I had a look at his hand. What kind of parents would let a young boy of that age get into such a state of infection." Staff Nurse Riley added.

Dr Novak nodded. "I'm afraid that lad also has more to deal with right now than the prospect of losing his hand to infection."

"Oh?" Staff Nurse Riley started to ask but was interrupted by a young male nurse entering the staff room hurriedly.

"Dr Novak," he said, breathless after his haste in looking for the woman. "The inspector has arrived. She wants a

2

word with you before speaking to the patients."

Dr Novak hurried down the last of his espresso and wiped his lips dry. "No rest for the wicked," He said and followed the young nurse out of the staff room.

~ ~ ~

Amanita

I don't know where to start. It was madness. I still can't get my head around it. We entered an alternate world – a realm spawned by grim fairy tales and horror stories. Elves, talking trees, and even Santa Claus himself made an appearance. It was one hell of a trip, one I was lucky to escape with my life, if not my sanity, intact. Jack, of course, was not so fortunate.

We did not do anything that countless thousands of other bored students haven't done before. It's just that we were unlucky in that the magic mushrooms we ate were ridiculously potent. These weren't the bog-standard small psilocybin mushrooms, you understand, the staple choice of escapist teenagers across the land. No, we chose something a little more avant-garde to keep us entertained for the evening. Jack discovered Fly agaric mushrooms growing on the Christmas tree plantation near the college. You know the ones – they're scattered throughout the illustrations of Enid Blyton storybooks. I think they drew them there to show that the world in which their characters lived was a magical realm of fairy tales. Think Noddy toadstools, and you will know the fungi. They were magical-looking toadstools, with large-domed red caps, peppered with white spots. Amanita muscaria, I think Jack called them, though they are also known as Fly agarics.

Why did we take Amanita instead of psilocybin? Firstly, it's the wrong season for psilocybin. With the high art-school student population in the area, those particular mushrooms have long since disappeared from our local fields. I don't think I have even seen any since late October. Secondly, though you may be unaware of this fact, consuming Fly agaric toadstools is a traditionally festive activity. Raise your eyebrows as much as you like because it is a fact. Even the supernatural figure of Santa Claus has its roots firmly planted in the psychoactive mushroom culture. Numerous studies show that the iconography and rituals associated with Father Christmas's mythology were stolen from psychedelic mushroom-consuming Siberia communities.

People there lived in teepee-like constructions made from reindeer skins, the rooves of which were supported by a large beam of wood that stretched up to its smoke hole, an essential feature designed for ventilation for interior yurt fires. During the Mid-Winter Festival, the chief shaman dressed in his ceremonial garb, a Fly agaric coloured red and white coat with fur trimmings and long black boots. There is no prize for guessing the similarity here with our familiar image of Santa Claus. The shaman then scoured the woods for Fly agaric mushrooms. Filling his bag with the magical fungi, the shaman would clamber up the yurt exterior and make his ceremonial entrance via its smoke hole. To the thrilled excitement of those in the community awaiting his arrival, the shaman would then slide down the central pole and share out his Fly agaric gifts with them. At the ceremony's closure, the shaman would leave the yurt by climbing the wood beam and exiting through the smoke hole again.

Even the magical reindeer who guide Santa Claus through the sky originate back from the Fly agaric's hallucinogenic properties. Siberian reindeer have a particular preference for the fungi and behave very oddly under their influence. Siberian communities even feed the reindeer the mushroom and later collect the reindeer's urine. The waste from these Amanita-fed animals not only retains the full hallucinogenic strength of the Fly agaric, but the reindeer's digestive process also reduces much of the toadstool's noted toxicity. With both the reindeer and the shaman inebriated, the reindeer's excited erratic behaviour often gave the impression that the animals were attempting flight. This effect of the mushroom, the perceived notion of impossible flight in wingless animals, provided the mushroom with its alternate title, Fly Agaric.

When Christian missionaries first entered Siberia to spread the word of Jesus, they saw the shaman's sacred rites and heard their stories of flying reindeer. And it did not take long before the customs and folklore of these indigenous people became intertwined with Christian Christmas traditions. Even Father Christmas' magical home eventually found itself relocating to the frozen lands of the north.

And so I hope you can see that what Jack and I did was just as much a part of Christmas as you going out and getting drunk at a Christmas party. Don't you agree?

Given that neither Jack nor I had an excellent home life to return to, we decided to stay on in our separate college halls of residence over the Christmas holidays and enjoy the festive season together. Neither of us had any actual plans for how we would occupy ourselves over the holiday. Nor had we realised just how boring it would be living in a student village when nearly all the other residents had deserted the place for a few weeks.

I held no romantic feelings towards Jack, and I don't think he thought of me in those terms either. He was excruciatingly shy, too reserved to make a pass at me, bless him, and I certainly was not looking for any romantic involvement with the guy. He was a gawky individual, a character who found himself at odds with the world around him. He was a decent bloke, though, and in no way deserved what happened to him.

Anyway, he first mentioned having discovered some unusual mushrooms, which he reckoned were hallucinogenic, a few evenings after all the other students had left for their family homes for the Christmas holiday. I was already bored at that point, so when he floated the notion of eating some, I readily accepted the invitation of accompanying him on his proposed trip of a lifetime.

Jack was into his wildlife, as well as his psychoactive mushrooms. And he seemed to have a thorough knowledge of the fungus in question. He explained why Amanita muscaria's popularity had waned amongst the contemporary counter-culture in favour of its fellow magic mushroom, psilocybin. It was the perceived, rather than the actual, dangers associated with the mushroom's consumption. Recorded fatalities resulting from misidentifying other Amanita species such as Amanita phalloides – the death cap – and Amanita virosa – The Destroying Angel, were rare, he assured me. That said, caution is necessary when preparing the mushroom for its entheogenic properties. To reduce Fly agaric nausea, users must first dry the mushrooms before consuming them. Jack said the act of drying the fungi both lowered its toxicity levels and increased the potency of its psychedelic compound Muscimol. As I said, Jack seemed to know his shit. He was aware of the dangers and how to offset them naturally. So, yes, I trusted him on the matter.

Anyway, one afternoon, when I popped over to his room to kill some time, Jack pulled a brown cardboard box from beneath his bed and, setting it between us on the mattress, opened it as though

11

he was unveiling some precious treasured artefact he was proud to show off. And there, within the box, lay three freshly harvested Amanita muscaria toadstools.

"They're beautiful," I said. "I don't think I have seen such mushrooms in real life before. I didn't even think they were real."

"Oh, they are real, alright." Jack enthused, broadly smiling as he studied the trio of colourful fungi before us. "Portals to new magical worlds, they are. I'm just drying them out now before munching down on them."

"They're safe, are they?" I asked.

"Sure, so long as you know what you are doing." Jeck smiled mischievously.

"Which you do?" I enquired.

Jack grinned. "Of course." He reassured me."

"So, when's the big occasion?"

Jack closed the box of magickal toadstools and slid it back beneath his bed. "Well, I'm going to try and follow the traditional shamanic method and ingest them on the mid-winter solstice. Amanita muscaria is recognised throughout the world as a sacred key into magical realms. Under their influence, partakers of this fungus have returned from their psychedelic trips, having conversed with gnome-like creatures who helped guide them through alternate dimensions.

"Gnomes, ey? So you get to adventure with fairytale figures when tripping on them?" I asked, genuinely fascinated, not to mention excited, by Jack's discovery.

"Siberian shamans believed that for each mushroom consumed, one gnome would manifest itself. The creature, summoned to a place, not of their liking, would immediately race back to its magical realm, allowing the shaman the opportunity to follow them to their psychedelic world. However, these squat earth-spirits could run as though the devil himself was chasing them. On their race through the convoluted passageways into their alternate world, the shaman would often lose sight of the more spritely gnome and, unable to find the entrance to their kingdom unaided, would return to their material bodies with no gifts of arcane knowledge or sage counsel from the wise spirits. And so the canny shamans would always consume one and a half Fly agarics at the start of their journey – one to enable their minds to see the gnomes and the half to conjure a weaker half-gnome creature. The conjuration of the less abled, slower halfling gnome would allow the shaman to follow the supernatural creature through the circuitous route to the Netherworld with no fear of losing their way."

"Interesting," I mused aloud.

"I was kind of hoping you would come along with me when I take the trip." He said nervously. "To share the experience with me."

I shrugged. "Sure, it's not like I have much else planned for that night." I laughed. "Round yours, is it?"

Jack shook his head. "No, I'm going to try and get the full authentic and natural experience from the mushrooms. We could head down to the woods near the area I found the mushrooms and take them there. Are you in?"

"I might be. I will see how *you* get on with the mushrooms first, though." I laughed.

"Cool," Jack smiled. "It's something for us to look forward to, eh?"

As the day of the winter solstice approached, I began to get quite excited about the evening's events. It had been quite a while since I had experienced butterflies in my stomach like that. I still hadn't finally made up my mind about whether I would just be minding Jack on his trip or whether I would be joining him in the whole psychedelic adventure. In the meantime, I researched the toadstool in the college library.

Ideally, I should have been studying for my dissertation, the first draft of which was due to be handed in at the start of the spring term, just a couple of weeks away. But, as it turned out, by the time I had finished my research, I had managed to work out how to use my art dissertation to explore the fascinating pop iconography of the infamous mushroom. Despite its negative press, the fungi seemed to offer quite an exciting experience for those brave enough, or stupid enough, to give it a try. I would, of course, be exercising caution by giving Jack a good hour and a half start on me with the mushrooms to gauge whether or not he was enjoying the experience before I committed to a decision.

15

The motif of Amanita muscaria, connecting it with the spiritual realm of elves and fairies and gnomes, surrounds us all to this day. Even the most conservative people bring a little of the Fly agaric's magic to their lives through the literature they read, the television programmes they watch, the religious festivities they follow and even the garden ornaments they purchase. Enjoyed by adults as much as children, computer video games also use the iconography of the Fly agaric mushroom, perhaps most memorably in the acclaimed Super Mario Brothers franchise where, upon consuming the magical fungi, the Mario Brothers gain superpowers and strength. Replica Amanita muscaria mushrooms, often displayed alongside guardian gnomes, also decorate gardens right across the world. It is difficult to imagine the weight of concrete and plaster used to create all of these faux psychedelic decorations.

I looked forward to the mid-winter solstice as it was a break in the boredom, which was surprisingly intense as the Christmas holiday dragged on. I had become lazy, laying in later and later until I stopped experiencing morning daylight altogether. On the day of the mid-winter solstice itself, I did not wake up until well after mid-day, and I did not drag myself out of bed until well into the afternoon.

The clouds were thick with snow when I finally made my way to Jack's, its weight so heavy hardly any sunlight trickled through its mass to brighten the day. Located on the other side of the college campus, it was but a ten-minute walk from my college dorm to Jack's, and I found him sitting outside of his hall of residence, backpack at his side when I arrived.

"You're eager," I said, with a smile as I approached.

"Sure am. It's going to be a wild night." Jack enthused as he rose to his feet, slinging his rucksack over his shoulder as he took a swig from his cheap super-strength can of lager. "Here, wet your whistle on this." He said, already walking away from the college accommodation grounds as he passed me an unopened can from his stash.

We took the back route through the rear of the college car park, now eerily barren - as though we were the only people left alive in the whole world. Clambering over the turnstile into the fields, we headed towards the woodland, where we were to set up camp for the day. As we made our way across our cold, empty pats, a soft pattering of icy rain began to spit. My face tingled as their flecks reached my face as though tiny slivers of glass were scratching my skin. "Looks like it may snow," I remarked, pointing at the leaden sky that loomed above the approaching woodland. "It's certainly cold enough to."

"Could very well do so." Jack agreed. "Don't worry, though. I've found ourselves a well cosy spot that will keep us dry."

I heard Jack's words with relief. I had not fancied experiencing the cold and wet woodland whilst tripping. I needed an evening of fun, not having to endure a full-blown bad trip forced on by uncomfortable surroundings.

A small brook appeared as we approached the old woods, and we followed its course amongst the trees until it led us to a small stone humpback bridge.

"I've already set it all up," Jack continued as he stepped over the tinkling stream towards the bank of dried mud and pebbles that rose from the water's edge beneath the bridge. "I popped over yesterday evening to save us time today." He pointed at the extensive collection of wood and twigs he had gathered together in a pile there. "It should be nice and dry now and spark up nicely." He said, motioning to a patch of flattened earth at the side of the fire-to-be. "Get yourself settled there and ready yourself for the ride of your life."

I looked about the scene, impressed at Jack's preparation. "Can I light it now?" I asked with a shiver.

Jack smiled. "Sure." He said and passed me a small box of matches. "Spark it up, and I can sort out the mushrooms."

I pocketed the matches whilst I rearranged the pile of twigs and wood, tidying the array of fuel into neat stacks, as much to give myself the impression that I had participated in organising the proceedings as anything else. Then, adding a few of their number to a smaller heap, I began work constructing our campfire. Finally, my fingers already raw with the cold, I retrieved the box of matches from my pocket, opened it and struck one alight.

I savoured the sound of the match dragging fast against the sandpaper and the scent of sulphur that rose from the small flame. This night was my most exciting evening for many a long month. And I wanted to experience every little nuance and sensation the occasion offered, no matter how fleeting. With an abundance of caution, I introduced the flame to the pile of wood and sticks I had arranged precisely before me. Three matches later, the campfire finally crackled to life, and I built its flames as fast as I could manage, finally mustering some warmth for my bones.

Settling himself before the fire, Jack passed me another can of lager as he emptied his own. Crushing his can as small as he was able, he popped it inside a carrier bag he had brought along specifically to gather the litter generated by our psychedelic endeavours. He seemed intent on getting off his face as fast as he could. Shrugging, I necked down the remains of my current can, tossed it into the refuse bag, and accepted his offer of a second can. Opening it, I took a large swig of its cheap and not quite appetising contents.

His thirst temporarily quenched, Jack unpacked a metal tripod from his rucksack. Placing the construction over the fire, he hung a metal pot from the chain attached to the tripod's apex and poured a fresh bottle of water into the bowl.

"You know," He said as he finally pulled a familiar-looking paper bag from his rucksack. "This place has a magical history."

"Oh, yes?" I replied, pushing my half-emptied can of lager into the stony earth at my side to stop it from tipping over.

"Indeed." He continued with relish. "The area is sited on the spot where three leylines cross – just over there." He continued, motioning with a nod towards the nearby fields on the other side of the woods."There used to be a stone circle sited over where the Christmas tree plantation now stands – the same site I found these precious mammas." He said, producing the three dried Fly agaric mushrooms from their bag.

"What happened to the standing stones?" I asked, my interest piqued. I had undertaken a little research on the area before I decided to accept my offer of a place at the Art College earlier in the year. But I had seen no mention of such history in the tourist literature I had poured through at that time.

21

"The villagers tore it down. Many years ago now. It gained something of a bad reputation and attracted bad sorts to the area. A girl from the village was found there in the end, killed in some freaky Satanic ritual. Local folklore said that the land there demanded sacrifices of human blood to enrichen its soil - something like that anyway. Anyway, no matter the truth, it makes for a good story. And it gives us something to think about when eating these mushrooms. It's not often that we get to eat magic mushrooms that the blood of sacrificial victims has fertilised." Jack laughed teasingly at the notion.

I watched, lost in thought for a moment, as he dropped two of the large Fly agarics into the pan of boiling water. Crumpling the emptied bag into a tight ball, he added it to the fire. A huge lick of flame consumed the paper dramatically. Breaking the remaining third Amanita muscaria into two, Jack offered me one of the halves.

"One each to get us to where we want to go," he said, nodding at the two Amanitas bubbling in the water above the fire. "And a half each to summon our halfling guides so that we can follow them into the underworld."

22

Watching him fold his half into his mouth, I followed suit and sat the fungi firmly on my tongue. I was doing this, after all. Though I would, of course, resist the other toadstool for a while after Jack had consumed his, I promised myself for safety reasons.

The toadstool felt dry in my mouth, its skin unfamiliar and wrinkled like a cold dead toad. Salty and savoury.

"Chew it slowly and deliberately before swallowing," Jack said as he munched down on his toadstool half.

The Amanita was spongy to the bite, and I consumed it as directed. Swallowing the fungi, I then waited patiently, content to drift off into whatever dreamy state awaited me as Jack now sipped eagerly at the mushroom tea he had brewed. Refusing, for now, a mug of the offered brew, we both sat silent as we waited for the effect of the psychoactive fungi to take hold of our minds.

After half an hour or so, I lost track of the passing time and, my thoughts became hazy, as though they bobbed serenely upon a tranquil pond. Although the day was heavy and grey, especially in the gloom beneath the bridge, I began to notice a kind of inner light behind the physical façade of the natural world about me. Just sitting there, before the small fire, it seemed a lovely sensation to silently watch the world at play beneath the ancient stone arch - the colours of the rocks, of the tangled vegetation and the various mosses that clung to the bridge's underside, becoming psychedelic in their splendour. The air that separated me from the outer physical world slowly began to flex, as though it was breathing, and the colour and sound shifts around me ebbed and flowed pleasantly in a gentle wave. As I sat there, enthused in the world that twinkled and entertained, I felt my sense of the ordinary and familiar fade, replaced by a curious appreciation of the magic of the phenomenological world. Things had taken on an *Alice in Wonderland* ambience, and time itself now slowed. I marvelled at the slow-motion descent of the snow and how sound itself stretched and distended about me. God only knew how Jack was experiencing things, having consumed a far higher dose of fungi!

The day gradually gave way to the evening of the shortest day of the year. It was dusk now, but our spot beneath the hunchback bridge was lit cosily from the campfire before us. For the first time in my life, I felt a feeling of total connectedness with nature, as though a final jigsaw piece of my understanding of life had suddenly slotted into place. My brain had overcomplicated what it should feel like to be alive. Now I understood the straightforward simplicity of it all, and I felt an extreme and profound sense of joy at being part of this marvellous universe.

"You know," I said greedily, aware of the enormous grin that had spread across my face. "I think I am ready for some of that tea now."

But Jack, lost in his thoughts as he waved his fingers to form patterns before our fire, paid no attention to me. His happy absorption in the activity made me jealous. I wanted more of the Amanita mushroom inside my system, and I gave Jack a nudge with my elbow, nodding at the pot of tea that still bubbled like some witch's cauldron alive with a magical potion.

Jack helped himself to another brew as he scooped my portion of the tea from the saucepan, and we smiled at one another like two naughty kids as we clicked mugs and brought the potent infusion to our lips.

We soon fell away to our bespoke phantasmagoria; the warm, dreamy mood spoiled only by nausea, dry mouth and odd periods of profuse sweating – the physical side-effects of the Amanita. But as the light from the world beyond the underbelly of our bridge continued to fade and dissolve into darkness, the bridge's deepening shade gave my skin a curious, intricate sheen that piqued my concern.

"Ay, I've never noticed it before. My skin looks kind of leaf-like." I expected Jack to laugh at my words, but he appeared suddenly excited and alert.

"Did you hear that?" He asked.

"The stream, you mean?" I asked.

"No. Something is starting to happen. Listen carefully," Jack instructed. "I think they are approaching."

The wood on the fire crackled sharply, but Jack shook his head dismissively when I suggested with a nod that this might be what he had heard.

Then I, too, heard the sound he referred to and knew beyond doubt that we were entering a new, more intense phase of our trip. My heartbeat sped as I concentrated on the sounds.

"Goblins will gobble you." The sound came again and appeared closer this time. And now, the atmosphere of our camp shifted dramatically. All semblance of reality retreated fast, as though it were a curtain, thrown back to reveal a crazy pantomime as our campsite transformed into the home of a troll, or goblin, or whatever fairytale characters headed down the stream towards us.

I turned to Jack again as I tried to ascertain whether my alarm was suited to the occasion. His eyes were wide - his pupil's blown huge like a sentinel owl.

"What are those?" I asked in hushed tones. "Should we get out of here?"

Far from evidencing the kind of fear that engulfed me, Jack seemed positively ecstatic by the arrival of the short shadowy beings. "Ready for action?" He asked as he clambered to his haunches, ready to leap to his feet.

The chattering creatures, racing along the edge of the stream, were beneath the bridge with us now. Unlike Jack, however, I perceived their raucous chant of "Goblins will gobble you" as an immediate threat to my safety.

"Jeez, how many of them are there"! I asked with growing alarm.

And then, illuminated by the light of our campfire, I saw them - twisted, tortured, hideous beasts, ugly as sin, their eyes, reflecting the flames as they approached, shining with a wild madness,

"What the hell are they, Jack?" I shrieked, panicked by their grisly appearance.

"They're gnomes. They are answering our summons." Jack answered, now on his feet. "Come on, get up. We have to follow them. Don't let them get out of sight."

The creatures were upon us in seconds, and as they raced past, I felt one of them brush against my body. And at that moment, in an increasingly rare moment of clarity, I realised the true identity of the 'gnomes'.

Follow them!" Jack screeched, himself already heading out from under the bridge in the chase.

"Jack, they're not gnomes. Look at them. They are turkeys, for God's sakes. They've probably escaped the Christmas slaughterhouse."

But, in a few maniacal bounds, Jack had already reached the top of the bank outside the bridge. And, ignorant of my elucidation, he ushered me to join him there.

"You are not going to believe what I am seeing." Jack panted excitedly. "I've lost the gnomes, but they led me far enough to know the route forward."

"They weren't gnomes." I tried to enlighten him again. I felt the need to keep him safe, to persuade him not to head off on a fool's errand. God only knew how this would end.

Jack ignored my explanation and waved for me to be silent. "I can see Santa Claus." He called back to me. "He's sticking the last Christmas tree in the field onto the back of his sleigh."

"What!" I exclaimed, clambering hurriedly to see what exactly was screwing with Jack's head so much.

Climbing up the bank after Jack, I peered over the top to view the magical delights Jack had detailed. Instead of Santa and his sleigh, all I saw was an older man in a red coat struggling with a Christmas tree he had just felled. I turned to Jack, ready to offer him a third reality check. But he was so entranced with *his* individual take on the proceedings that he ignored my words as if they had never even passed my lips.

We watched the guy sling the tree onto the back of his truck and then disappear into the front cabin of the vehicle. At that moment, with the driver out of sight, Jack raced onto the field, engulfed in his enchantment.

"I'm going for a ride on Santas's sleigh." He called back as he legged it over the snow towards the truck.

"Jesus." I groaned. This night was not proceeding at all as I had envisioned. Now it appeared the evening would culminate in an altercation between Jack and the truck driver. Jeez, his head must be well and truly gone, I reasoned, with a frisson of further panic as I wondered upon the extraordinary sights that lay ahead for me once the mushroom tea absorbed fully into my bloodstream!

To my astonishment, Jack turned out to be nimbler than I had ever imagined him to be. Reaching the truck, just as its engine started, Jack leapt, apparently unnoticed, onto the back of the vehicle, .just as it pulled away from the field, There, he secreted himself away by crawling and hiding beneath the cut Christmas tree on the truck's rear. And then they were gone, and I found myself alone and astonished.

I raced after the truck, following its trail in the freshly falling snow. The tracks were clear, and as the field led to a quiet country lane, it was an easy task to follow the vehicle's route from there. I followed the trail for only a little while before I found Jack, lying crumpled in a heap in the middle of the road.

"Jack, are you alright?" I called, ploughing through the deepening snow at speed now. The snow was red with blood about his crooked and still body. But I saw his eyelids flicker as I approached, and his fingers twitched as they tried to reach out to me for help.

I took Jack's hands in mine and cautiously hoisted him to his feet, checking to see if he could stand safely before releasing his hands from mine. He wobbled for a moment, then took a few steps forward, wincing as he did so.

"I don't think I've broken anything." He grimaced as he staggered forwards.

"Here," I said encouragingly. "Let's get back to the camp and collect our things. I think it's time we called it a night. Are you sure you don't need to get to a hospital? You've lost a fair bit of blood, you know!

Slinging his arm around my shoulder, I allowed him to lean his weight against me as I supported his hobbling frame back along the lane.

"How are you feeling?" I asked. "Mentally, I mean, not physically."

"Strange." He answered.

"Still hallucinating?" I probed a little further.

Jack shrugged. "If I am honest with you, I'm not sure what's real and what isn't anymore,"

"I don't think those were gnomes we saw earlier." I tried to rationalise with him again. And it was with some relief that I heard him agree. His reply, however, soon told me that he was still far away with the fairies.

"Yeah, I worked that out for myself." He whined. "They were elves. Christmas elves!"

"You still believe that was Santa's sleigh you climbed onto the back of?" I continued to probe his mental state gently. "You know I saw something completely different to your experience this evening?"

"Oh, Jess," Jack argued. "It was incredible. I have had a truly magical experience. I still can't believe it."

We were at the entrance to the empty Christmas tree plantation now, and the chilly breeze, wrapping itself around our bodies, tightened its embrace until we both started to shake visibly.

"You know," Jack said. "It gets to the stage where the cold eats holes in your body, until you become invisible to it, part of it even. And then there is a sense of true peace – a feeling of oneness – of transcendence."

We were in the centre of the field now, and Jack came to an abrupt halt, jarring me by his sudden stubborn immobilisation.

"What's wrong?" I asked, wondering if Jack had suffered some kind of concussion after being thrown from the back of the moving truck. My diagnosis was difficult to ascertain, however, given the state of his psychedelic intoxication.

Steadying himself, he held on to my shoulders and stared me directly in the eyes. His saucer-like pupils seemed glazed as they stared at me unwaveringly. "I'm just trying to gather my senses, Jess. I have a lot to process. That Christmas tree on the back of the sleigh, He said, deadpan. "It was alive."

"Jack, it takes a long time for trees to die after they get cut down, Jack." I tried to explain. "They hold so much water in their trunk, you see?

But he did not see. And he continued to stare at me as though it was I, not him, who was spouting pure gibberish.

"No, I mean it was *alive* – sentient. It communicated with me. Gave me a message - an instruction."

"It spoke to you?" I asked, hardly believing what I was now hearing and wishing Jack would come down from his trip and finally see sense.

"Yes. Well, it kind of did. It's hard to explain. But, whatever, it made its wishes, demands, known to me in the few moments I spent with it."

"Demands?" I asked nervously. Just how much further out of hand would tonight get? I wondered with growing distress. The look on Jack's face announced that I should pay particular attention to what, exactly, the Christmas tree had supposedly told him.

"It explained to me the importance of honouring the land, worshipping it even. We are all creatures of the soil. We shouldn't steal from and abuse what Mother Nature has given us. Our disrespect for the source of all life has been a crime. And amends need to be made. We must evidence the honour and reverence we once all gave to the land."

"What do you mean exactly, Jack? Are you saying that the tree gave you a lesson to be more environmentally aware? Did it tell you to go join the Green Party or something?" I asked, trying desperately now to lighten up his deadly earnest demeanour and wishing to God that he would sober up soon.

"A price has to be paid, Jess. Tonight. Now." He continued.

35

"A price?" What exactly are you saying, Jack?"

"A debt has to be settled for what has been taken from this land tonight. A life for a life!"

"*A life for a life?* What are you saying? Jack, you are talking crazy. Listen to yourself for a moment. Come on now. Let's get our belongings and get back home. Okay?"

"No, Jess. I am serious. Deadly so." Despite the darkness, the strange look developing in his eyes was startling to behold. "Don't be concerned, Jess. I am happy, happier than I have ever been in my life." Jack stopped and looked down at his feet, motioning with a nod of his head for me to follow suit.

The snow around his feet was dark with blood, Jack's injuries more severe than I had earlier dared to admit.

"I've been promised something extraordinary, Jess." Jack continued, breathless with excitement. "By surrendering my body to this soil, by feeding the land with my nutrients, I will be reborn into the wild plants that grow and takes nourishment from my blood! I'm to become one with the land, Jess. Do you understand? It's the Christmas gift I wanted most in the world – the peace of belonging."

Jack stumbled as though some force from beneath the earth had suddenly tugged at his feet. A moment later, blood gushed from his mouth, some internal injury from his fall from the truck abruptly making itself apparent. "It begins." He gargled triumphantly.

"Quick, Jack. Give me your hand. We need to get out of here fast."

Jack withdrew his hands from my aid and held his arms high to prevent me from trying to haul him from the soil and snow. "No, Jess. I want this." He said, jerking as his legs sank deeper into the field, up to his knees this time. As he dropped, he vomited a gut -full of blood over the pair of us.

"Jack, there will probably be another Christmas tree planted in this field. You'll be cut down and killed again in less than a year. Stop this dangerous nonsense and come with me. Now!."

"No." Jack shook his head adamantly. "There will be no more commercialisation of this land."

"Jack, seriously. You need to straighten up and be rational. Now, before it's too late." The stench of blood and vomit made me want to wrench myself, and I knew that I, too, needed to make a rapid escape from the field.

"The farm this land forms part of has come to an end. It will soon cease trading. There will be no more plundering of this sacred land by those greedy and stupid enough to try and make a monetary profit from nature. The land, this field, will finally be allowed to revert to its natural state of being. It will become a sacred place again. As part of that land, I will survive for hundreds, even thousands, of years – at one with the earth and the world."

"No, Jack. You have to stop thinking like this before it goes too far."

"Why don't you join me, Jess? Share this gift of an experience. Be at one with nature and me." Jack suddenly plunged further into the ground, and now the entire length of his legs was swallowed by the earth. "Take me!" He cried in exaltation.

There were no further words from Jack. Just a stream of dark blood dripped from his open mouth before it, too, was swallowed by the field.

"No!" I shrieked, retreating fast now as Jack was consumed wholly by the field.

And then there was silence. And I slowed my breathless escape to take a glance at the land behind me. There was no sign of Jack now. The earth had swallowed him entirely. The falling snow had even covered the blood the guy had vomited, as though conspiring with the land to disguise Jack's murder. I stopped, breathless. Exhausted, I felt suddenly sick -another bout of mushroom nausea blending with the stench of Jack's blood on my clothing. And then I vomited, throwing what appeared like the entire contents of my stomach onto the virgin snow before me. Aghast at the sight of my half-digested mushroom tea and lager that sullied the white sheet of snow before me. I screamed when I saw *my* blood stained the vomit at my feet. What the hell was going on? The blood and vomit sank into the snow like acid through plastic, and when I tried to step around the mess, I found my feet suddenly pulled to their ankles into the ground.

"No!" I screamed, terrified of being consumed by the land like Jack. The earth had enjoyed the taste of his body and now wanted more." I looked around as I sank to my knees in the field, desperate to spot anyone who could help me. And then I saw him, in the distance but approaching fast – a peculiar figure racing across the field to my aid - a little Christmas elf...

Dr. Novak stood by the door of the single hospital room, holding the door ajar to hurry the Detective Inspector from his questioning of his patient. At last, she concluded the interviewing session and stepped out of the room with the doctor.

"I take it you have run a full toxicology report?" The Detective Inspector asked as Dr Noval closed the private room door behind them.

"Of course." Dr Novak confirmed. "The results won't be back from the lab until the morning, but it seems like standard muscinol poisoning to me. We've given her charcoal tablets and pumped her stomach to be on the safe side, but there is no evidence to suggest she has taken anything other than Amanita muscaria mushrooms, along with a little alcohol. That particular species of mushroom is noted for its profound hallucinogenic properties, as well as its deliriant effect, both of which you have witnessed for yourself in the patient's statement to you." Dr Novak stated confidently. She should be fine when the effects wear off. Perhaps if you

41

return in the morning, you may get a more lucid account of the night's proceedings." He suggested.

The Detective Inspector nodded thoughtfully. "Perhaps." She answered non-committedly. "Though I will want to speak to her again. I take it you won't be discharging here before I get to speak to her again?"

Dr Noval nodded silently.

"Good." The Detective Inspector continued. "Though to be on the safe side, I'll post an officer outside her room tonight."

"Is that really necessary?" Dr Novak asked. "She's hardly in a state to discharge herself, you know."

"Still, best to be on the safe side. This is a murder investigation after all. And we wouldn't want one of our prime witnesses walking out of here before we get a clearer statement from her"

"Murder?" Dr Novak queried, surprised by this turn of events. "So you believe the girl's story about her boyfriend? Have you found a body?"

"I can confirm that a couple of bodies have been found, doctor. However, neither body was that of a teenage male."

"Oh?" Dr Novak asked, intrigued now as well as surprised.

"Indeed. Though the girl is not the prime suspect, she is a person of interest."

"So have you any idea who the murderer is?" The doctor tried to dig past the inspector's poker face.

"The young boy. Is he medically fit to face some questions?"#2the boy?" The doctor asked, confused. "Surely he is not your suspect in a murder investigation? He is only nine years old!" But the inspector waved away his curiosity.

"May I question the lad?" She asked.

The doctor nodded. "Sure thing. He may be a bit woozy with all the painkillers we have pumped into his system, but he's lucid enough for you to interview him. Should I call in his parents? We haven't been able to locate them yet, unfortunately, but…"

"That won't be necessary, doctor. We have a duty solicitor on her way and they can sit in on the questioning in place of his parents."

Dr. Novak nodded. "Follow me, then." He said and led the Detective Inspector to the young patient's hospital room.

~ ~ ~

Gobble

As a monster, this will be difficult for you to understand. I can sense you possess that grim delectation for corpse-munching so typical amongst your kind. For some reason, carnists seem content for their bellies to become the graves for all the poor animals that are tortured and killed so that they can enjoy the taste of their decaying flesh. carnist's guts are part of the crime scene of horror and carnage of an industry you seem happy to promulgate. If you eat meat, then you are a monster. And your blind nonchalance or faux-ignorance to this fact makes no dent in the accusation I place on you gluttonous, self-serving monsters. Yes, I've used that word again – monsters. For that is indeed what you are.

Would you be happy if you went home tonight to find someone in your house had sold your pet cat or dog for the butcher's table? Or your wife had taken them out to your garden shed and slaughtered them for your supper? What, exactly, is the difference between a cat or a dog or a cow or a pig? Or a turkey? All take joy from the warmth of the sun. And all have a love of play. All take solace from feeling safe. Pigs are more intelligent and emotionally sensitive than any dog. Did you know that fact? Do you even care? But I bet you anything that you would not eat a dog, would you? This demarcation of yours, between the animals you want to kill and eat and the ones you welcome into homes like surrogate children, is a fallacy. They eat dogs in some countries. Your culture invents that difference to give you a supposed, yet illusionary, moral compass to murder those unfortunate souls who find themselves on your list of animals you have defined as 'food for your belly'. These poor, desolate souls suffer cruel and shortened lives whilst you pamper the pets you supposedly 'love'. Aha, I can see in the flicker of your eyes that you are starting to understand my argument. Good for you, monster. For you know, deep down, don't you, that *you* are the real monster here? Not me.

Do you know the natural life span of a turkey is ten years? Have a guess how old farmers allow their turkeys to live before they kill them. Sixteen weeks, on average. And during the very few weeks they are allowed to live, they are overfed to ridiculous proportions – until they reach twice the weight of an adult bird in the wild. Turkeys are kept receptive to overeating by raising them beneath intense light for long periods of the day and night. The light is so fierce that it actually damages the bird's retinas and can blind the poor souls. Did you know that? Do you care? Maybe, I guess. But certainly not enough to do anything about it, of that I can be confident.

Am I sorry for what I did? My reply to that particular question is that I'm disappointed that my actions became necessary. All life is precious. But to save life demands extreme measures, especially if you are fighting against a world of uncaring monsters. Which I was.

So, you want me to start by telling you everything from the beginning? I'm happy enough to do that if you have the time. I'll begin on the morning before the mid-winter Solstice, from when I ran up to the Christmas tree plantation to check that Father had not broken his promise to me.

A painful stitch in my gut forced me to slow my pace as I ran through the field towards the Christmas trees. I could hear the chainsaw ripping through the last crop of trees there, decapitating them from their roots. The late Christmas market for trees must have been strong this year, I guessed. The din of the chainsaw made me furious, it being anathema to the natural sounds that should resonate through the countryside. I felt sick now, but on I continued, following the stream that crawled beneath the humpback bridge in the fields below the plantation.

I turned sharply and clambered up the incline that made a shortcut to the Christmas tree field on the far side of the bridge. Halfway up the slope, I panicked as the chainsaw fell silent. Was I already too late?

By the time I reached the plantation, the pickup lorry was already loading the freshly felled trees. Climbing up onto the field, I studied the view before me, my pent-up anger making my body tremble in rage. Half the plantation had already been cleared for the pre-December market, and now the final patch of trees was being felled. I watched Father and the lorry driver netting up the trees and loading them onto the rear of the lorry. Seeing me, Father waved, calling me over to join him near the truck. I, however, was in no mood for family niceties, and I crossed the field with a mission to make my feelings fully known.

"Remember, you promised to keep one of the trees for me," I said, reaching Father, who was passing another felled tree through the netting machine to be collected for market by the lorry driver.

"Your mother did mention something this morning," Father replied. "Was there a particular tree you wanted or will any do?"

I rolled my eyes. I thought I had already made plain to Father the tree I wanted to save. Thank God I had reached him in time. "It's the best Christmas tree in the field," I said. "Mum said you would save it for me and let it grow for another year. She said you'd already agreed to it as a Christmas/birthday present for me."

Father sighed. "I thought you were hoping to save one of the turkey's lives this year as your birthday/Christmas present?"

"Toni, the turkey is for this Christmas, Dad. The tree will be for next year's present. Anyway, does that mean you will allow me to keep one of this year's turkeys then?"

Father ruffled my head lightly. "I told you, I can't promise anything about

50

the turkey yet. It all depends on orders. At the moment, there are five birds left on the farm with no further orders for them. So far, so good. But you know we are struggling with money on the farm. Business will have to come first, I'm afraid." Father noticed the disappointment on my face and ruffled my hair again. "But the Christmas tree, I *can* promise you. Here, come and show me the tree you've fallen in love with." I noticed Father's attempt to put an arm around my neck, but I hastened my pace to avoid his touch. I was annoyed at him for cutting down the woodland. And he had commenced felling them before finalising which tree I wanted preserving from the chop. Money mattered more to the man than the life his land sustained, which grated massively on me.

"This is the tree," I said as we finally reached the Scottish pine.

"Damn Noel, you've gone and chosen the finest tree I've ever grown on this plot. " Father laughed, half-heartedly. "Okay, consider this one saved for another year," He said. "Now run along and let me get back to work."

Mother gave me a concerned look as I walked back into the farmhouse. She was on the telephone, and her voice quietened as I closed the front door and, out of view, began to ascend the stairs to my bedroom. Something was up. I knew it instinctively. Stomping on the stairs, I lightened my weight on the same step to give the impression of going up to my room. However, halfway up the stairs, I sat down quietly to listen to my mother's conversation.

"So that's five birds you want to be delivered. Okay, we can do that for you, Mr Bentley. That will be the last of our turkeys then for this Christmas."

I blinked hard, barely believing what I was hearing. My parents were going to sell Toni and her remaining sisters! I simply could not let that happen. Quietly, I tiptoed the rest of the way to my room, where, after closing the door quietly, I flung myself onto my bed and began to cry.

Father yelled when he got home for his tea. "The boy has to learn that we work on a farm. We aren't living in some kind of Walt Disney film! This vegetarian nonsense of his has to stop. And stop now."

I listened to Father's brutish words in horror and disdain. What kind of man was he? He'd spent today killing dozens of trees, and tomorrow he would blithely put to death the last five turkeys they had remaining on the farm – Toni being one of them!

"He says he's a vegan. Not a vegetarian." Mother corrected him.

"Whatever he says he is, it's over. Cook him up a proper breakfast tomorrow. Bacon, sausage and eggs. Let's get this silliness over and done with for once and for all."

That night I sleepwalked. Not for the first time, I know. But this time, I was semi-conscious – like a dream from which I was slowly awakening. I found myself visiting the local woods. There I made my way through the tangled undergrowth to reach the old ruined church walls, long overgrown with a thicket of ivy. There was another plant growing there too, which in the summer sported glossy black berries but now lay crisp and dying with the progress of winter. With no tools, I knelt before the ancient altar there and dug my bare hands into the soil, digging deep to unearth the wizened plant's roots. The experience was vivid yet dream-like. The only reason I knew my woodland exploits had actually taken place was that when I woke up the following morning, I found my hands caked in dry mud, and I wondered but did not investigate whether the rest of my night's dark deeds had been part of a dream. However, I was soon to discover that they were not.

Instead, I hurried down the stairs quietly, straight out to the turkey shed, the scent of mother's deranged cooking reaching me despite the stench of turkey dung. Mother had obviously chosen sides and had put up camp firmly in enemy territory. The stench of pig flesh, being fried on the kitchen hob, turned my gut and made me hunker down on my plan for the day. The dice were cast. It was time for me to take action, to set things right on the farm - for once and for all. A lesson would be taught today. And what a day for change to establish its course – the mid-winter solstice! Decision made, I lifted the latch on the door to the turkey shed and stepped back into the farmstead, leaving the door ajar. I smiled as I stepped away as I heard the last clutch of turkeys suddenly start gobbling, their interest in their possible escape route piqued. This was going to be a very interesting mid-winter solstice on the farm.

Hearing movement at the front door, I snuck down behind the turkey shed, quieting my excited breathing as much as I was able so as not to give my hiding place away. A moment later, the door opened, and mother stepped out into the daylight.

"Noel. Your breakfast is getting cold. Come inside now - it's on the table. Hurry, Father and I want a word with you too." A short pause as she realised the turkey shed door stood ajar. "Jeff, you'd better get out here – the turkeys are loose!"

"How did they bloody get loose?" Father moaned at top volume from the kitchen.

Mother turned, disappearing indoors again, pulling the door shut behind her. "I don't know. But you'd better get out there and sort it before they make a mess of the yard." Her voice, muffled now, grew softer and more distant.

Now would be my best chance, I reasoned. Get the turkeys out of sight before Father came blundering out to recapture the birds. Knowing the man's temper, he would probably execute Toni and her remaining sisters as and when he caught them, using the traditional and gruesome neck-stretching method.

I was out from behind the turkey shed in a shot, and clapping my hands as softly as I could so as not to alert my parents and still make the impact needed, I began to herd the turkeys, at speed, away from the farmhouse.

Toni and her sisters were not afraid of me because the birds and I had formed friendships over the short few months of their lives. But this made the task of shepherding the birds to safety difficult as they were not scared of my approach. Instead, they crowded around my feet, pecking at the dirt there in search of treats. Luckily, Father was slow to leave his beloved breakfast of dead pig, and I managed to disappear into the hedgerow and the field beyond before he staggered out onto the front porch.

"God damn it! You left the door unlatched when you fed the turkeys last night." He called back brusquely to Mother.

"No, I didn't, Gordon. I don't like the damned birds. They are ugly as sin and give me the creeps. There's no way I would risk them getting out. Especially when I know you'll be getting rid of them all today."

"Well, someone let them out." Father continued. A short silence as his mind ticked over the issue. "Noel. Get here now!" He yelled.

I did not budge. The turkeys were exploring the hedge in the far corner of the field now, well out of sight of Father. I waited for his next move, daring not to make a sound.

"Jesus, there will be hell to pay for this, Noel! Do you hear me? If I find out you let those damned turkeys out, there will be no Christmas celebrated in our house this year. Do you hear me?! And you can say goodbye to that stupid tree you fuss about up on the top field. Come out here this instant, or, I swear, I will cut the thing down this very morning!"

I remained still but could not help but let a smile cross my lips. Though Father did not know it, he would not be cutting my tree down that day. Nor would he be killing Toni or her sisters. Of that, I was confident.

I waited until I heard the front door of the house slam shut behind him as he returned angrily to his breakfast. I then headed up to the top field myself to pay another visit to the magical Christmas tree and the Lady of the Land, who had promised me in last night's pseudo-dream would be awaiting me there.

"You finish your breakfast, Father," I whispered. "Gobble it all, and don't forget to wash it all down with some nice fresh coffee." And with that, I raced back across the yard to head up to the top field.

Always reliable, The Lady of the Land, dressed in her usual pale blue hooded robe, stood by my Christmas tree, which now stood alone and stark in the field now the other trees had been harvested for Christmas. The Lady of the Land seemed to be in a quiet conversation with the tree, whose needles bristled in the wind as though communicating a response to the Lady's words. Hearing me approach, she turned to me, lowering her hood from her face and head as I approached.

"Is it done?" She asked solemnly.

"They were drinking it when I left to free Toni and see you," I answered. "Are you sure it will work?"

The Lady of the Land nodded. "It will work – if you followed my instruction."

I can see your interest in the Lady of the Land is piqued. Your brow furrows, and your eyes thin every time I mention her. Oh yes, she is real enough, I assure you. She and others who work with her will become the new guardians of the sacred land – and will become my guardian at the appropriate time. Anyway, where was I? Oh yes.

"I've let Toni and her sisters free. I couldn't stand seeing their little faces caged up in there, knowing what Father had planned for them later. I know you said that they would be safe, but I had to take precautions. "

The robed lady waved away my concerns. "Your turkeys will be safe. As will the other animals on your farm now." She said. She held out a hand, offering it to me. I accepted and slipped my small hand within hers. Her fingers curled over mine and were warm and comforting. "Come," She smiled reassuringly. "Let's attend to matters and secure this land for our future."

The farmstead was quiet as we approached the house across the yard.

The landrover, quietly parked by the gates, told me Father was still in the house. My fingers tightened onto the robed lady's hand nervously as we continued to the front door of the house.

At the door, we stopped. "You sure about this?" I asked.

The Lady of the Land nodded. Reaching out, she knocked at the door. After a long silence, she knocked again. From the kitchen came the sound of something crashing to the floor. Then silence again. "It's okay." She smiled at me. "Do you have a key to get back in?"

I pointed to the empty milk crate in the corner of the yard. "There's a spare key under there," I answered, already making my way across the yard to collect it. Lifting the dusty metal crate from the ground, I picked up the key that lay hidden beneath it and wiped the thing down from dust and dew on my jeans before slotting it into the keyhole. Here goes then." I said, turning it and feeling the lock mechanism clunk open. Retrieving the key, I placed it in my pocket and pushed the front door ajar.

Now, at this point, I have to admit to you that I was a little unsure of what I had allowed to happen. But, I remembered the pact I had made in the presence of the great tree. My promise to protect it had been solemnised in blood by the drawing of one of its sharp branches across my palm. How could I forget the ritual whilst a large sprinter from the tree remained stubbornly beneath the wounded skin? Despite its growing soreness there, I had been unable to shift the thing from my hand and now just hoped that it would one day work itself free from my flesh. Whatever was to take place on the farm that day was for the greater good.

Cautiously, I made my way down the quiet hall towards the kitchen, my heart thundering as I wondered what I would find there.

Father was still sitting at the kitchen table, his eyes wide and staring – his pupils huge in the centre of their glazed orbs. Mother lay sprawled on the floor at the side of the table, the chair overturned. She lay motionless. Dead. Father must have noticed my presence as he gurgled something unintelligible through his stilled lips.

"He knows we are here." The Lady of the Land said. "The deadly nightshade roots you mixed into their coffee this morning will have blurred his vision, made him extremely sensitive to light. His heart will be beating fast, thundering in his ears like a funeral drum. He will find it difficult to distinguish hallucination from reality. But he will be able to hear us. Do you have any last words for him?"

I did. My hand began to throb as I turned to address my Father. Seeing his eyes flicker in my direction as I approached, I smiled at him. "Gobble down your coffee, did you father?" I asked, stepping closer. "I knew to add the powdered root to the coffee as mother always drinks more of the stuff in the morning than you. And I didn't have a lesson to teach her, not as great a one I have to teach you. So I knew she would receive a dose that killed her kindly. There was no need for her to suffer unduly. Not such a quick ending for you, I am afraid though, Father."

Father's dry lips, already starting to chap and crack as they swole, moved silently. His mouth and throat, too dry to speak, instead issued forth a slurred groan.

"Enjoy your breakfast, did you? What is it you had? And what a waste for you not to finish your meal. If you only knew what suffering went into that meal, you could have at least made an effort not to waste it. Oh, but you do know, don't you? Indeed, you are the cause of so much of it." I glanced down at his still unfinished meal. "A little piggy, I see. What else? Egg. Do you know the horrors committed just so you and your sad kind can eat chicken periods? You disgust me." I spat in a fury at the helpless man before me. And then I caught that particular look in his eyes, at the knowledge of his impending demise, that I had seen so often in the cows the old man had sent out to slaughter over the years. Curiously, I noticed that in my sudden vitriol, the pain in my throbbing hand subsided. "And what is this you have served me here, Father." I continued, enjoying the easing of my pain. "More pig and poached chicken periods." In a moment of anger, which surprised me as much as it obviously did my Father, I waved the untouched plate of death and suffering from the table. As the plate smashed against the wall, smearing animal fat and grease down across its surface as it fell to the floor, my Father jerked and began shaking visibly in his chair.

"He's fitting." The Lady of the Land told me. "Quick, let's get to work before it's too late for him to savour the kind of suffering he has committed in the world."

Lifting him from beneath his arms from the chair, the Lady of the Land motioned me with a glance to take hold of Father's legs to help carry him. Instinctively, I knew where we were taking him – to boil in the broth of his own creating. Before he finally shuffled off this mortal coil, he would endure at least a fraction of the suffering of the animals he had raised so others of his kind could savour the taste of their flesh on their tongues. He made me want to vomit.

I know what you are thinking. I can see it in your eyes. But you're mistaken. I am no sadist, no matter what your narrow view of the world leads you to believe. But I will not go into any of the gruesome details for your amusement of what happened to Father in his slaughterhouse. I will leave you to discover that for yourself if you haven't already done so. I just hope that your tastes aren't too rich, as I'm afraid he might be a tad overcooked."

Anyway, I suppose you want to know what happened afterwards, with the girl? When our work was over and the Lady of the Land had left to make the final preparations for her evening's work, I went in search of Toni and her sisters. I followed the path down from the field where I had last seen her, which then led me beneath the old bridge at the bottom of the Christmas tree plantation. I imagined they had made their way up to the top field as it seems to attract a lot of wildlife up there, and I wanted another chance to visit the last remaining tree there too.

It was dark and snowing now, and I saw by the tracks in the snow that I was not alone. I wondered if the Lady of the Land had passed this way, so I hurried up the bank to the top field, where I heard voices. Human voices.

When I reached the edge of the field, though, I soon realised that it wasn't the Lady of the Land who awaited me there or any other of her coven. The promise of their acquaintance and eventually joining their number was, as yet, unfulfilled. Instead, a couple of stupid teenagers presented themselves to me. The pair stank of fear of what was proceeding, so I knew they were not partners with the Lady of the Land.

At the time, I thought they were right to be fearful, for they had defiled the night's intended proceeding by chopping down the sacred tree, which was to be the integral centrepiece for the night's ritual. But when I later spoke to the girl, she told me it had not been them who had slaughtered the mighty Scottish Pine tree. By then, of course, it was too late to save the boy. He had already been sacrificed to the land. However, there was no need for the girl to die also. I am not a monster, you see, and I knew by her scent that she, like me, was not a corpse-muncher. Her respect for life granted her life. It is the way of things.

Don't look startled by the term corpse-muncher. Isn't that what your kind genuinely are? Isn't that what you like to feast on – the dead flesh of murdered animal corpses? And, yes, non-corpse-munchers can sniff out the carcasses that rot in your belly. Its rancid decay carries on every breath you exhale.

Is the girl okay now? I hope so. The world needs more of our kind.

Can you please call the doctor back in to see me? My hand, you know, it hurts really bad. Look at it. It's almost black from infection. The doctor said he would try his best to save it, but I don't know. Do you? He says that the infection may have affected my mind, the blood poisoning having caused me to think delusionally. He said that explains what I did to my poor parents. I don't know. I have been ill these past few weeks. My parents neglected me to the degree that my hand was allowed to get into this shape. Perhaps people will look kindly upon my actions when they hear of the abuse I suffered at my parent's hands – brutalised and nagged to consume the dead flesh of tortured animals. It's enough to make anyone crack, especially a young boy, I suppose. Anyway, as I helped her to her feet and tried to calm her hysterical behaviour, the familiar gobble-gobble sound of Toni and her sisters sounded close by, and I left the girl to pick and hug the turkey.

The girl's eyes looked off, as though she witnessing more of her environment than I had initially given her credit for, and I realised that she was in some kind of shamanic trance. In time, when all this was over, we might reach out to that one, and invite her into our circle. She has a lot to offer our community.

And that is that. There isn't too much to add to the tale, not from me anyway. The girl found a signal on her mobile phone and called for an ambulance. When I saw the flashing lights of an ambulance and a police car, I let Toni free, kicked some snow gently at her to encourage her to flee and, given the state of my putrefying hand, was brought to this hospital with her.

Anyway, listen, if my hand does get chopped off, why don't you ask for it? Why would you want it? To eat, of course, silly. I'm sure it would go down well with your chips for tea tonight. And I am pretty sure that you needn't pull that face. I am sure you have already eaten a lot worse. Please, get the doctor and let me rest now. I have no more to say.

"Back again." Staff Nurse Riley said. "I don't think I've even left the hospital over the past week." The nurse answered.

"I know how you feel. Anyway, Merry Christmas." Dr Novak said, lifting his cup of freshly poured Espresso in salute.

"And a Merry Christmas to you too." The nurse answered, raising her cup of coffee in response.

"Quiet evening?" Dr Novak asked.

"I wish," The nurse sighed. "It's been a bit of a repeat of the winter solstice night here this afternoon. Seems like there's no end to the funny business going on at Solstice Hill. I've heard the police inspector is on her way back to the hospital. I take it you know about the new patient?"

"No." Dr Noval admitted, straightening his hair at the thought of meeting the Chief Inspector again. "I've only just started my shift. I just needed a coffee to set me up for the night ahead."

"You will be needing, doctor." The nurse advised. "Something weird has been going on that god-awful hill." She repeated herself. "What with the disappearance of that young student boy and the young kid killing his parents. And now we have another case."

"Another case?" The doctor arched an eyebrow inquisitively.

"Another patient who has been up to no good near that farm at the bottom of Solstice Hill. You know that whole area has quite the history, don't you?"

The doctor smiled, waving away the nurse's superstition. "Oh, you mean the rumours of devil-worshippers, witches and things that go bump in the night?" He laughed. "Yes, I've read a little on the history of the place. What's the connection between the farm and this new patient?"

"The silly bugger only went and chopped himself down one of the Christmas trees that were growing on Solstice Hill."

"And?" The doctor encouraged the nurse as he emptied his cup of coffee and threw the polystyrene cup in the bin.

"Well, he only went and chopped off one of his own hands!" The nurse exclaimed.

"I hardly think we can link everything that happens over at Solstice Hill can be linked to its dark pagan history." Dr Novak reasoned.

"I agree, doctor. But the thing is, this old gent said he'd got a splinter from the tree he chopped down stuck in his hand – just like that little kid who killed his parents the other day. The old fool said he believed he was being possessed by the spirit of the tree he had chopped down and said he had to chop off the infected hand before the spirit directed the hand cruelly against his young daughter."

"I see," Dr Novak mused on the strange tale. "You said the Inspector was on her way to speak to the guy?"

The nurse nodded.

"Then I think I will take a look at the patient before she arrives."

The nurse put out a hand and rested it tenderly on the doctor's forearm. "Go careful, doctor. I don't like all this talk of spirits and possessions and the like. It gives me the right heeby-jeebies."

"I'll go careful, I promise." Dr Novak smiled and left the room in search of his curious new patient.

~~~

Thursday, 23 June 2022

Your driver Sammie will deliver your Amazon parcel today between 15:31-16:31, you have options if you are not in www.dpd.co.uk/b/9K33dugPEQ

09:04

The Dryad

With the ignition turned off, the freezing air began to creep inside the truck. The cold prompted me to take a nip from my whisky flask to warm my bones a little before I set off across the field. Tucking the flask back inside my jacket pocket, I undid my seat belt, opened the door and stepped out into the night.

Fastening my jacket against the chill of the night, I consoled myself with the thought that I would soon be back behind the wheel and driving home to a warm fire. Hurrying to the back of the truck, I retrieved my long-handled axe and the old oil lamp I had brought along to illuminate my work. Striking a match, I delicately introduced its flame to the blackened wick. The smell of kerosene rose in the air as the lamp's soft glow flickered in the breeze before finding its life. The light brought the falling sleet into sharp relief and made the scene appear as though it stood within a giant snow globe. The small pellets of sleet thickened as I watched them and had already started to settle on the ground. The cold made me groan, and I took another nip from my hip flask to help me on my way. Savouring its effect, I swung the large axe over my shoulder and strode out across the field.

I listened. Only the sound of the wind and my own feet as they crunched over the hard soil broke the silence as I made my way out to the solitary tree that awaited the swing of my axe. As I had hoped, there was no one else around to disturb me or intrude upon my work. It should be an easy matter to get away with the robbery. Nevertheless, I wanted to work fast, get the job over and done with and head back home where I could relax in the warm again.

The tree I wanted to claim as my prize for heading out in the cold and dark was a Scotch Pine, which happened to be the finest specimen of a Christmas tree I had ever seen. It first caught my attention earlier that day as I had driven past the field en route to the local shop to collect my weekly groceries. It had stood out, growing alone in a lot that, just the week before, had supported over a thousand of its number. Now, viewing the tree at close quarters, I was left curious as to the reason why it, alone amongst the plantation, had not met the bite of the forester's chainsaw.

Resting my axe at my feet, I lifted the lamp high in the air and swung it around slowly to regard the tree at close quarters. The plantation owner must also have noticed the uniquely fine qualities inherent in this tree to have spared it from this year's Christmas market. He must have decided that it would fetch a more substantial price if given an extra year's growth. Maybe he had even earmarked the tree for his own home the following Christmas. That would no longer happen, as this perfect Christmas tree would now be adorning my living room before this night was through.

Lowering my lamp to the ground, I lifted the large axe again and readied my aim for a clean and precise swing Only the chop never came. The axe hung heavy in the night air, poised but hesitant to do its master's bidding. It was an odd sensation and one I did not particularly appreciate. You have to understand that I am, or was, a craftsman by trade, and it was essential that I maintained a sure hand when directing my tools. Uncertainty was anathema to my work and something I could not countenance. I can't honestly find the accurate words to describe what I felt, but it was as though the tree did not want me to strike it down and was actively trying to persuade my axe to rebel against my instruction. The axe felt heavier in my hands than I have ever remembered it being before, and my fingers felt clumsy around its haft. Suddenly dizzy, I brought my axe to rest, leaning its long handle against the trunk of the tree as I took a moment's pause to steady myself.

"Come on now, Joseph. Steady yourself." I scolded myself aloud for my hesitation. Little Annie would have been so disappointed in me had she woken up in the morning to discover that I had still not sorted out a tree for her. Promising her a Christmas to remember, taking home this Christmas tree tonight was the very least I could do. Any action I carried out to ease the psychological trauma of Annie's first Christmas without her mother was worth my effort. I had already left it as late as December the twenty-first, the mid-winter solstice, to procure myself a tree for our home. And here I was, still hesitating to do my duty to what remained of my family.

"Don't get your hopes up," I warned my adversary resolutely. "I haven't finished with you yet. I'm just taking a short rest, that's all. I must have taken a bigger slug on that whisky than

I'd intended. But you will be on the back of my truck soon enough."

The tree rustled in the breeze as if responding to my dark promise. The sound caught my ears like the whispering of some ancient, unfathomable language.

Damn it, what was it about this tree that made it so difficult for me to cut it down? Already spared once this Christmas, it now felt almost cruel of me to want to take the tree's life. I shook my head to rattle the ridiculous notion from my head.

"Oh, stop grumbling." I mocked the tree gently in an attempt to raise my spirits against the rasping sound produced by its nodding branches. "Isn't your purpose in this life to become a Christmas tree? Look around. All your friends and family have already left. You don't want to be alone this Christmas, stood out in this field in the wind and snow. There are no others of your kind here to shelter you now. You will feel every gust of wind, every bite of the cold. Your perfect shape will be corrupted by the winter storms to come. No one will admire you then. Best you come with me now, whilst you are in your prime, eh? I'll take you home to my daughter, where she will love you. God knows she needs some cheer in her life right now. Come with me now, and I will decorate you like the splendid specimen of a tree you are. I will dress and adorn you with pretty glittering baubles and trinkets and shining garlands of gold and silver tinsel. How fine you will look." I reasoned with the tree in an attempt to reduce my growing guilt at taking the tree's life.

The tree bristled in the breeze again, and I could not help but imagine I heard words issuing from its jostling pine needles.

"What's that you say, tree? It is an honour for you to accompany me home this evening?" I feigned the tree's response, knowing in my heart that the tree did not want to lose its life to the blade of my axe. It wanted to live, as much as my dear wife had wanted to live. But as her wishes had been ignored by whatever God had decided upon her cruel fate, I too would overlook this tree's desire to be left alone to grow in peace.

A hoarse whisper left the branches of the tree, borne from a wind that had suddenly picked up to a gust and shook its branches briskly. I listened, mesmerised by the sounds its swaying

81

branches produced. It was a curious thing to think, let alone repeat here. But, for a moment, it seemed that I heard the tree say. "Leave me. Go home. Forget me."

I shivered. Looking back, I can't honestly say whether it was from the cold of the wintry night or from the creepy effect the tree was having upon my senses. Also, at that moment, disquieting me further, I no longer felt alone and that some unseen presence in the ancient woodland behind me was studying my every action. The feeling was so real I turned to catch the interloper but saw nor heard no one and I quickly grew annoyed at my growing paranoia.

"Enough!" I said, aloud, to underline my determination on the matter. "This nonsense has to stop." I would fell this tree, right there and then. I was sick of being made to feel the monkey and would stand it no longer. As if in response to my proclamation, the wind whipped about me with sudden force. The branches of the tree waved angrily in the gusts, and my axe, which had been resting amongst them, toppled forward, the tip of its bulky haft catching my shin bone as it did so.

I swore and hopped in pain and cursed the tree then. Fuelled by revenge for its assault upon my person, I reached down for the axe. Taking it in my hands with both relish and vigour, I raised the blade high above my head. Swinging the axe back, I prepared the blow that would bring a close to the night's nonsense.

Again, weariness overcame me, and my axe felt burdensome in my hands. "To hell with you!" I grunted, ignoring the feeling and, with all the strength of mind and body I could summon, I brought the full weight of the axe cracking down into the base of the fir tree.

Two odd things happened in the instant my axe cut into that infernal tree. The sound of the blade as it bit hard into the trunk thundered across the field with a shocking volume. A shadowy mass of distant, disgruntled woodland birds lifted en masse into the sky as the sound echoed through its tangled thicket. The second strange happenstance that occurred was that the wind, which had built to strong gusts in the last few minutes, died instantly upon the impact of my blade upon the tree. The solemn silence of the stilled air gave extra weight to the sound of the axe - the absence of the wind so swift and dramatic that its departure seemed a direct reaction to the tree's injury. Prising the blade from the wounded tree, I stood quietly and listened. The silence about me was now profound. All I could hear was my heart as it thudded in my chest. I waited a while for my heartbeat to settle and for the birdcalls to start up again. To my discomfort, neither occurred.

"Enough." I finally cried, and I took a second solid swing at the tree. Again the sound of the splitting collision of steel on living wood sounded like a sonic boom in my ears. Ignoring my giddying thoughts, I rapidly prised the blade free from the tree and followed through with my assault with a third and immediate fourth blow.

Now, I am a man used to hard labour. But felling that tree left me panting like a man unused to physical work. But, finally, drained to the core, I dragged my axe from the trunk and watched as the tree, decapitated from its roots, creaked and toppled and fell to the ground. The deed was complete. Mission accomplished.

And with that, the sound of an owl tooting brought the night back to life and the stilled air ruffled with a small breeze once more. It felt as though, with the felling of this tree, I had awoken from a state of trance. And it was a relief to return to reality. Checking my watch, I confirmed that I had dallied there on the plantation for too long and I needed to get home fast to relieve the babysitter from her evening duties. And so, without any further ado, I lobbed my axe into the back of the truck and set to work dragging my prize fir tree across the brittle field towards the vehicle.

I opened the truck door and clambered into the driving seat with more than a sense of relief that the job of cutting down the tree was complete. God only knew what had come over me. I guessed at the time it had been all the stress of Christmas, thrown into sharp relief by the death of my wife earlier in the year. Having Corrine pop into my head again, a tear welled up in my eye. I could not afford to think of her right now. I had to keep my grief and depression at bay for my daughter's sake. I had to make it through this first year intact if I was going to stand any semblance of a chance of making Corrine proud of me. And of raising Annie to become an accomplished, strong, independent woman, like Corrine herself.

Brushing my cheek dry, I checked in the rear-view mirror to see that the emotion of the moment hadn't manifested on my features, not wanting the babysitter to notice my sadness. But as I rubbed at the swollen eyelids, I stopped dead as I heard something heavy shifting its weight in the back of the truck! At the same time, a light suddenly appeared in the field behind me. Fearing that it was the forest ranger, hell-bent on halting the theft of his prize tree, I turned the ignition without further ado, pushed the truck into gear and sped from the scene towards home.

It would have been so much easier for me to have bought a Christmas tree for Annie! But my finances had been more than tight since Corrine had passed away. She had been the one to hold down the regular full-time job that had sourced our monthly family income. My work, crafting and selling wooden furniture and gifts, provided a more sporadic and less reliable wage. And I had been unable to put my mind to work in recent months after her death. I had still not got round to making the doll's house I had planned for Annie's Christmas present. The little money I possessed was required to keep a roof over our heads and to put food on our table. That said, I would have to pay the babysitter an extra half hour's pay for my delay. Still, I reasoned, the babysitter was the teenager daughter of my wife's best friend and only charged a modicum fee for her services. Perhaps I could get away with an apology instead of an increased payment.

Relieved though I was at managing to snag my free tree, I could not shift the tense, unsettled mood that had fallen upon me during its procurement. And these resurfaced with a vengeance when I heard another bump from the back of the truck. The tree had suddenly jerked as though I had driven at haste over a speed bump. Checking the rear-view mirror for any possible animal roadkill I might have left in my wake, I saw the road behind me lay as barren and flat as it was ahead of me. The sound and movement had indeed originated from the tree and not my driving. Perhaps a squirrel remained secreted away amongst its branches and had shifted the weight of the tree as it scurried around in a confused frenzy? Only the bump I had heard appeared to have been made by a creature much more significant in size than any squirrel I had ever encountered.

The shuffling sound came again and, glancing back at my cargo, glimpsed the tree shifting its position in the back of the truck. It was as though it were trying to escape from the vehicle. As my eyes fixed on the shadowy scene, the tree became suddenly fixed in situ, leading me to question my sanity once again. Only a few minutes from home now, I resolved to ignore any other sound or movement for the rest of the journey. Thankfully, however, there was no repeat of the strange occurrence.

The babysitter, evidently impatient for my return, came rushing from the house in her coat and gloves as I reached my ramshackle cottage.

"Sorry." I apologised as I hurried from the truck. "The job took longer than I had envisioned."

"No worries," Samantha answered politely. "I was getting a little worried you might have gotten caught up somewhere in this snow."

"In this baby?" I said, motioning proudly to my truck. "No fear of that happening."

Samantha smiled. "Anyway, I'd better get home."

I pushed a crumpled ten-pound note into her hand, the fee we had agreed on earlier. "Sorry, it's not more." I apologised again. "You know it's been a tough year."

"Honestly, don't worry about it." She shrugged. "It was nice getting some peace from my brother's loud music. He knows I can't abide heavy metal and I swear he plays his horrendous music at top volume every evening just to annoy me."

"Annie has been good for you, then?" I asked.

"Yeah, she got her head down early. She's excited about seeing the Christmas tree in the morning. I see you got one then." She added, peering into the back of the truck.

"Yes. It's a beauty too. Do you think Annie will like it?"

"I'm sure she will." Samantha smiled, not giving the tree the kind of awe I thought it deserved. "You look a right Santa Claus in this snow with that red coat of yours." She laughed. "Anyway, I'd better get off. Have a good night, Jo."

"Yes, I guess I must have stood out. You have a good night too." I returned, nodding appreciatively. Crossing the road to her family home, she waved goodbye as she stepped inside and closed the front door behind her.

Alone in the driveway, I turned my attention back to the Christmas tree, half expecting some large squirrel to be still secreted away amongst its branches. Lifting the tree by its severed end, I gave the whole thing a shake. Apart from the white flurry of snow that fell as a fine powder from its branches, all was still when I finished. Whatever creature I might have inadvertently loaded onto the back of my truck along with the tree must have leapt from the vehicle somewhere during the drive home.

"Right, let's get you inside, buddy. It's not as bad in there as you might have feared. You may even enjoy the experience" I spoke in jest to the tree. I often talked to the items of wood I sawed and chiselled and sand-papered and shaped into new forms in my work shed. It's a lonely life being a carpenter, and talking to inanimate objects had become a habit. And one I instantly regretted continuing as soon as I spoke those words to that damned tree.

Despite my friendly welcome, numerous splinters stabbed into my hands as I hauled the tree over my shoulders from the back of the truck. Now I had gotten splinters innumerable times over the years. It went with my trade. But these particular splinters were nasty, spiteful things that dug deep into my flesh and stung like poison.

Dragging the tree into the house, I left it propped up in the corner of the hall as I locked the front door and went upstairs to attend to my injuries. Clicking the bathroom door closed softly behind me, so as not to disturb Annie's sleep, I pulled on the bathroom light and removed my coat, guiding its arms gingerly over my splintered hands so as not to aggravate my injuries. I grimaced as I regarded my hands carefully beneath the bright bathroom light. The tree had got me good and proper. There must have been more than a dozen fragments of dark bark in my left hand and a half dozen more in my right.

Being a carpenter, my hands are relatively immune to pain. But, my affected fingers stung as they rattled through the various bottles and boxes in the bathroom cabinet as they searched out my wife's old tweezers. Eventually locating them, I began the task of guiding their pointed ends into my flesh, in search of each sliver of wood that had embedded themselves there.

The pain of the procedure was unusually intense, which I put down to my hands softening from having spent less time in my workshed this year. And, whilst I could easily slip the majority of their number free from my palms and fingers, one remained stubbornly embedded in my left hand, its removal requiring more agony than I was able to endure. Cursing, I returned the tweezers to the bathroom cabinet. The splinter would have to work its way out of my flesh a little before I made another attempt to remove it. Dabbing the blood from my stinging hands, I returned downstairs and, more cautiously this time, manoeuvred the fir tree from the hallway into the living room, ready for its decoration.

As I swung open the living room door, Benjamin, my old cat, let out a screech as though the devil itself was on its tail. In a state of terror, he arched his back as he hissed and spat at the tree. He tried to make a swift exit from the room, but the tree blocked and frustrated his escape. In desperation, Benjamin tore around the room in scatty circles, screeching and climbing the walls in fear.

"Hush Benjy," I tried to soothe the cat, who was now a ball of hackled fur. But he seemed oblivious to my attempts to appease him, his fear of the tree sending the old cat crashing into the ornaments that lined the windowsill and mantelpiece as it climbed the walls and spiralled around the room. Fearing that he might suffer a heart attack through his distress, I heaved the tree into the living room as quick as I could manage and stepped aside to enable the scatty feline his escape. Benjamin immediately tore past me, skidding down the hall as it raced towards the kitchen. A second later, I heard the cat-flap in the back door swinging to and fro. And that was the last time I ever saw my twenty-year-old cat, who had been a trusted companion to me for all of my adult life.

The evening's toil was starting to take effect on me now, and I felt the first stirrings of weariness settle in my bones. And so, with a fair amount of work to get done that night, I pushed my poor puss cat from my mind. I needed to concentrate on the task at hand – setting up the Christmas tree so Annie could see it in its full glory when she awoke in the morning. And, after adding a few coals to the fire to warm the room, I set my mind and hands wholly to the task.

Progress on the tree was slow and made painful with the injury in my left hand. I cursed the tree repeatedly as I secured it to the Christmas tree base and started decorating the infernal thing. The fairy lights were a dawdle, but I was annoyed at how unsteady my hands were at the task of attaching the bells, baubles and other small glittering trinkets to the tree. Even making allowances for my tiredness, I was annoyed at how shaky my fingers were as they went about their work. As I have already noted, I pride myself on my steady hands. Indeed, they are a prerequisite for success in my craft. But now they trembled. The incessant sound of the tiny Christmas tree bells, tinkling as I dressed the tree, began to irritate me too. They jangled in my head, and I was concerned their clamour might wake my daughter. I blamed the lingering soreness of my remaining splinter for the instability of my fingers. And, in an attempt to calm its discomfort, I used a short break from my task to quarter fill a glass tumbler with whisky. The drink, however, failed miserably to soothe either the pain or my mood. Especially so when, whisky cupped gently in both my hands, I regarding my decoration of the tree. Untouched by human hands, the numerous little bells, spread neatly amongst the fir's branches, started tinkling away at me again!

Fear rose in me, I won't lie, as my mind desperately fought for a rational explanation as to an explanation of the tinkling bells. Had Benjamin found a little bravery in those old bones of his? Had he returned to the household to sharpen his claws on the tree in an act of dominance? Alas, my hope for a rational explanation was unfounded, and I finished my whisky in haste. Using Benjamin as an excuse to leave the room, I went to the back door, opening it to call out to the missing cat. It was still snowing, its increasing depth having already erased his small paw prints from the garden path. Reluctantly, I closed and locked the door again, hoping Benjamin would make it through such a bitter night. Refilling my tumbler with another shot of whisky, I returned, with real trepidation, to the living room.

Thankfully, the tree stood quiet and still when I entered the room. Taking a quick slug at my liquor, I placed the glass on the mantelpiece and turned to study the tree afresh. Perhaps I had imagined it all. Maybe my hand had been so shaky the tree had taken a few moments to steady itself after I stopped dressing it. I tried desperately to convince myself of a rational explanation as, gathering some more baubles, I returned to my work, still intent on completing the Christmas tree before retiring for the night.

I don't know how much longer I dressed the tree that night. But I do know that I did have a couple more slugs of whisky during the process. And it was only when the effect of the alcohol began to take effect on me that I took, what I intended to be, a short rest on the settee.

Oblivion, however, swallowed me without warning once I laid down. And I did not awaken until the following morning when the sound of the Christmas tree bells' constant jingling jarred me to consciousness. Horror broke an immediate sweat on my brow, and I sat bolt upright to face the tree. Thankfully, the sound turned out to have no imagined supernatural cause and was, instead, created by my daughter completing the job I had been too drunk and tired to finish myself. However, my relief did not last long. "You're up early, Annie," I said as I squinted at Annie through the daylight that beamed in through the living room window.

"You woke me up." She answered, as she carefully placed another bauble, a small brightly coloured red and white mushroom, on one of the last undecorated branches of the Christmas tree. "You were making a right racket, Daddy. You woke me up with the sound of jingling bells. I thought Father Christmas had come early. I have nearly finished decorating the tree for you now, Daddy. I just have this last decoration to add."

Annie pulled a small wooden figure of Pinocchio from the now emptied decoration box and went to hang it from one of the lower branches of the Christmas tree. As she went to hang the ornament, however, the tree suddenly toppled over towards her. I swear, the thing fell on top of my daughter of its own volition. I had, without a doubt, placed the tree squarely in its base the night before. And the thing was perpendicular and as evenly hung with decorations as was humanly possible. And yet the damned thing fell and crashed right on top of my daughter!

I rushed from the settee, uplifting the tree to pull Annie to her feet. Her little body trembled as I held her at arm's length to regard her injuries. Thankfully, she seemed fine, just a few cuts where some of the Christmas baubles had smashed on their impact with her. Having picked the odd piece of plastic shrapnel from her pyjamas, I ruffled her hair reassuringly. "There, nothing but a few scratches. And it looks like you might sport the odd bruise or two tomorrow." I made light of the accident. Annie nodded, bleary-eyed, and I could tell by the way her eyes continually darted between me and the Christmas tree, that she was now very nervous about the thing. "You go and play upstairs now, whilst I get the tree in order and make it safer," I told her.

Annie blinked hard. "Okay." She agreed. "But go careful, Daddy." She warned. "Make sure you fix the tree properly in its base this time."

I nodded and watched her leave the room, listening to her small steps fade as they climbed the stairs. Was she blaming me for the tree falling on her? I wondered. Damn. It was correct that the thing had overturned without her actually touching the tree. I looked down at my empty whisky glass. Had I really relapsed my attention to safety when setting up the tree last night?

"Where's Benjy?" Annie asked later that morning as we sat eating our lunch before the roaring fire.

Glancing at the tree twinkling innocently, I decided to lie to my daughter. I was nervous about heightening her anxiety and so refrained from explaining that Benjamin had been so terrified of the Christmas tree that he had fled the house. "He's out enjoying the snow, Annie," I said instead. "It's a rare thing for him to see such a snowfall. He's making the most of it." Annie smiled at this. Perhaps I was a good father after all. "Eat up now. I want to see a clean plate." I said, motioning to the pile of uneaten green beans with a smile.

I spent the rest of the afternoon watching Annie playing with her dolls, whilst she sang Christmas carols at the top of her voice. I was still recovering from my hangover but did not want to stop her fun by getting her to quieten down. And so I remedied my malady by pouring myself another whisky to aid my banging head. The hair of the dog always worked wonders for me.

Throughout all the time she played, I saw Annie often glance nervously at the tree. Finally, she asked, "Daddy, are you sure there isn't some kind of animal still living in the tree. Its branches keep moving. Only, when I turn to look at it more closely, it stops."

I gave her the best reply I could to calm her worries, but could not help but feel that my assurance was unconvincing. "It's the heat from the fire, Annie. Try not to worry. It's just the tree drying out. It's like the noises the house makes as it settles in the night - the creaking stairs that used to frighten you - just the sound of wood settling to a change in heat. Remember those pine cones you and mum brought home last year? How do they open and close? It's the same principle. As the branches dry, they shrink a little that's all. It's that which gives the impression of movement. Don't be afraid of the tree, Annie. Let's enjoy this Christmas, eh?" And for the rest of that day, the two of us did our very best to do just that.

That night, however, after I had settled Annie into bed and I sat alone drinking in the living room, I became unsettled with the tree once again. The sound of branches swaying in a breeze suddenly filled the room. But when I scrutinised the tree in detail, I could detect no movement from it whatsoever. And yet, I could still hear the rustling, whispering sounds emanating from the tree. And, as I listened, I became convinced that the tree was trying to communicate with me And not only that. I imagined that I could interpret its words!

There, I have said it. I am as mad as might have been suggested to you already by my tale. But I did honestly believe that the Christmas tree was telling me that it was thirsty. And to assuage its need and quieten its nagging, I poured water into the base of the tree stand. Enough until the room fell quiet again and all I could hear once more was the crackle of the fire in the hearth.

After that, the tree grumbled whenever I spent any time alone with it. At first, its demands were just for more water, moaning that it was desperately thirsty. But soon the complaints included the room being too hot, demands that I stop putting coals on the fire and that I open the window to give it more air and that it needed more light. Its nagging became incessant and, to escape the constant pleading, I began to make excuses to spend less time in its company. Or even in the house itself.

The snow had fallen deeply over the past couple of days. And I used the changed magical veneer the countryside had gained over that time as an excuse to take Annie on longer and longer walks to explore this new winter wonderland. It was after one of these more prolonged walks, as I placed mine and Annie's damp clothing on the clothes horse before the living room fire to dry, that the Christmas tree voiced a new concern.

"I am lonely, Joseph." The tree bristled. "I miss the company I enjoyed in the forest. Even you and Annie are now avoiding me. I have not much life left in me now. I can feel my spirit fading as I speak. Please, Joseph, don't let me spend my last few days alone."

Now, before you ask, I was not one hundred per cent confident whether this was the Christmas tree speaking to me. Maybe it was just an extreme manifestation of some internalised guilt of me having stolen the tree. Perhaps it was an early sign of a mental breakdown. After all, I have been through some pretty nasty life-changing events this year. But I needed to silence that nagging voice, be it in my head, or not. And so I encouraged Annie to spend more time with me and in the living room in the company of the Christmas tree. She was still nervous about the tree, however, and could not spend long in its company before her anxiety made her return to her bedroom to continue her play there. And, left alone with the tree once more, its communication with me escalated.

On Christmas Eve, the tree told me, "I have not got much time left now, Joseph. I can feel my spirit fading. I cannot bear becoming firewood. Having found no friend to mourn my passing or remember me fondly, please do me one favour, Agree to my request, and I will forgive you for this torture you have inflicted upon me these past few days. Promise me, Joseph. Promise me."

And the Christmas tree then made its last request known to me. It wanted me to fashion its wood into a small doll, one that Annie would love and cherish for years to come. I knew that the tree was all but dead already and that Annie would not miss the tree if I took it down immediately. I had still not constructed her doll's house so such a gift would certainly make up for her scarcity of Christmas presents this year. And so I agreed to the tree's request. And, undressing it from its burden of decorations and fairy lights, I took the thing out to my workshop.

"Are you still in there?" I asked the tree spirit as I held the doll I worked on in my left hand.

"I am still here, Joseph. Use your skills to fashion me into as fine and lovable a creation as you are able. Finish your work before I die so that I may know what form will remain of me when my spirit fades. Let me behold how beautiful and how loved I will be forever. Be quick, Joseph." The wooden figure advised. "My time is short. Here, let me show you how to fashion me. Let me guide your hands, ease the burden of your will upon the wood. You can still turn the horrendous Christmas around for little Annie. Give her something to show her how much she is loved. With my help, you are still able to make this a Christmas Annie will remember. Just allow me to guide your hands."

And so I did. I could fight its will no longer. I allowed the spirit to slip into my hand and felt its presence in the sting of the tree's splinters that remained embedded in my flesh there. Taking

104

another swig of whisky to distance me from the pain, I allowed my hands to work upon the figure, independent of my direction. Finally, as the sun turned the evening sky golden, I made my way back towards the house with the completed wooden figure clutched tightly in my hand.

Heading into the living room, I hurried to wrap the present, genuinely believing it to be the most beautiful toy ever crafted. It would salvage our Christmas and Annie would love and cherish the gift. Of that, I was confident.

"Are you still there?" I asked the doll quietly before I enclosed it completely in wrapping paper.

The doll's reply was weak and tremulous. "I am. I will try to hold on until the morning. I wish to see the joy in little Annie's face when she looks upon me before I leave this world forever."

With the figure wrapped, I began sorting out the room, ready for Christmas morning.

When Christmas Day finally arrived, I relished the sound of little Annie tiptoeing into my room.

"Can we go downstairs and see if Father Christmas has been?" She asked when she saw that I was awake. Her eyes were wide with excitement. I had not seen her this happy for a long time.

I nodded, enthused at the thought of her unwrapping the doll that awaited her downstairs. And together, we went down to the living room.

"The Christmas tree has gone," Annie exclaimed as we entered the room.

"Oh, I didn't think you liked it," I answered as I poured coals onto the fire and got the flames to catch around them slowly. "Still, who needs a Christmas tree, eh? It's being with someone you love and getting presents from Santa that makes Christmas." Finished with the fire, I turned my full attention to Annie. She looked surprised and thrilled at the small collection of presents that lay where the tree had once dominated the room. "Go on, Annie." I encouraged her with a smile. "Tuck in."

Tentatively, and quivering with enthusiasm, Annie began to unwrap her Christmas gifts. There weren't many for her to open. The babysitter and her family had bought her a pretty little pink dress. Annie's grandparents, on her mother's side, had given her a teddy bear. And my parents had given her some picture books, a box of sweets and a jigsaw. Looking up from her presents, she smiled happily, as though they were the most precious gifts ever. Now it was time for her main present.

With a widening smile, I produced the gift from the mantlepiece."And this present is from me." I beamed at the anticipation of seeing the delight on little Annie's face when she saw what I had spent the previous day crafting for her. "Take it. I made it for you out of the wood of the Christmas tree. Go on, take it. Unwrap it. You'll fall in love with it as soon as you see it."

At the mention of the Christmas tree, Annie was suddenly nervous again. And she held back tentatively from taking the present from my hands. I could feel my irritation begin to rise now. Here I was, offering her what I believed to be the best Christmas gift ever, and she was making this fuss about the wood used in its construction!

"Here," I said, more curtly this time. "Take it. I made it for you, Annie. You'll adore it as soon as you set eyes on it, I promise. I put a lot of time and effort into making it for you. Don't be ungrateful. Take it quickly as I need to get the turkey in the oven if you want a Christmas dinner as well as presents today."

Annie, although afraid, finally reached out and took the present from my fingers. "But the Christmas tree, Daddy?" She complained quietly, stopping when she saw my reproachful glare. But my pleasure and pride returned as I watched Annie's little hands finally pull the wrapping paper from the wooden doll. And then I froze, in shock, at her reaction to my precious gift to her.

"Daddy!" She screamed, dropping the small wooden figure to the floor in shock. "It's horrible. Why would you make me such a scary thing?"

Anger at her ingratitude flooded my head at her outburst. And in a moment of fury, I lashed out at Annie. I promise it was the first time I ever hit her. "You ungrateful little..." I growled as my hand sailed across her face. The slap was hard, way too severe to be aimed at a child of her age. The blow sent Annie reeling backwards, where she lay sprawled out still on the carpet. A myriad of dried pine needles, which I had been too lazy to clear up fully the day before, surrounded her small body. Adding to my shame, I did not attend to my injured child but instead crouched to retrieve the wooden doll that lay at her feet. "Are you still in there?" I asked the figure apologetically. "I am so sorry about my daughter's reaction." But then, for the first time in days, I had a moment of real clarity. Repelled by the horror that suddenly confronted me, I held the figure at arm's length, shocked at the creation that affronted my sensibilities. Far from the perfect, beautiful doll that I had convinced myself it to be. I had instead crafted a hideous and vile demonic effigy. The thing was the most wretched and evil-looking abomination I could ever have imagined. And though it was not I who had conceived the monstrosity, it *had* been crafted by my hands. Hands I had once been so proud of, now shamed me for having brought such a vile, wicked thing into existence.

"Is this your true form, wood demon?" I demanded an answer, shaking the blasphemy before me. And in response, the wooden figure cackled aloud and maniacally.

I tossed the thing onto the fire then, repulsed by the lurid manifestation of corruption that confronted me. But my wait for the insane laughter to turn to anguish and pain as the flames licked hungrily at its urine and bile-coloured paintwork and slowly consumed its detestable form was in vain. The raucous laughter continued unabated as the effigy gradually became nothing but blackened ash. At that moment, I felt a sickening thud of pain in my left hand, and I looked down at the throbbing torment to discover that my left hand was a swollen mess, red and ripe with pus. How had I ignored that splinter from the Christmas tree that now festered so terribly in my hand? And as the laughter reached its hysterical crescendo, I realised that it was I who was laughing like a mad man. Whatever demon had made its home in that accursed Christmas tree, had transferred itself into the splinter embittered in my palm and was slowly taking possession of my whole body.

Panic-stricken, I saw Annie still lay quiet and motionless on the floor. But I had something urgent to attend to before I could help my poor daughter. Leaving her unattended, I raced from the house to my shed. The demonic laughter that spilt from my lips and the surging pain from my throbbing hand was too much for me to endure now. And I turned my attention

110

to my hand in the same fashion I had turned it to that tree on that god-awful winter solstice night. And, in an instant, I brought my axe down upon the atrocity that had become of my hand, severing it from my arm in one mighty and savage blow.

Leaving the axe embedded in the wooded workbench, I quickly grabbed a can of paraffin. I wanted to pour the flammable liquid onto the amputated hand and set it alight and destroy the demon for all eternity in the ensuing flames. But the severed hand was no longer there at the side of the axe blade. Horrified, I turned and followed the trail of blood, which led from the workshed, across the snowy path, and into the house towards Annie!

Dr Novak made his farewell and left the man resting in his hospital bed. As he stood gathering his thoughts outside the door of the hospital room, he glanced up as he heard someone calling his name. It was the Inspector, accompanied by a young, besuited gentleman, whom the doctor recognised as the city duty solicitor.

"Can we speak?" He asked the Inspector as she reached him outside the patient's hospital room door.

"Of course, doctor." The Inspector agreed. "It will give Mr Harvard time to speak with the patient."

Separating from the young duty solicitor, Dr Novak led the inspector away from the hospital ward and to his small private office room. With the door closed behind them, the doctor slipped the lock, ensuring the couple's discretion.

"A problem?" The Inspector asked, removing her coat and hanging it on the coat stand as she made herself at home in the office.

"What's going on here?" The doctor asked, taking a seat at his desk. Opening a drawer, he produced a bottle of gin and two empty glasses. The Inspector nodded her approval. Taking a seat opposite the doctor, she took the filled glass offered to her.

"Jesus, what's going on up there on Solstice Hill?" The doctor inquired. "The crazy shit that keeps happening there just keeps piling higher and higher!"

The Inspector smiled reassuringly at the doctor. "It's a bit of a long story." She said. "And one that would keep both you and me from our duties."

The doctor nodded, finishing off his drink in disappointment at the lack of more clarity.

Noting his disillusionment, the Inspector smiled again and tilted her head coyishly at the doctor coyishly. Perhaps, however, if you have the time this evening, we could meet up to discuss the situation?"

~ ~ ~

The Good Doctor

He stood in absolute darkness. The ice-cold ground beneath his bare feet stung and he concentrated on the faint warmth he received from the women who stood on each side of him. Their fingers, held tight within his palms, offered the only solace from the freezing night air. His body shivered, it's suffering at least numbing his mind from the circumstance of the night and the ominous part he might play in its grim unfolding. As he had been instructed, there was always solace to be found in pain. A small distance before him, a struck match sparked the central bonfire life, illuminating the scene before him in red. The grip on his hands tightened and the women on each side of him quickened their breathing in anticipation as the arcane proceedings commenced.

He studied the circle of naked, or skyclad as he had learned was the correct nomenclature, bodies about him. Their nudity neither stirred nor embarrassed him. Being a doctor, he was not shy of exposed bodies and understood the merit of its occasional necessity. Through their disrobing, the coven became a team that operated outside the normal parameters of the mundane world. And in this particular instance, nudity served to bring the coven closer to the elements they all believed could be controlled.

Admittedly, that first skyclad ritual, held on the night of Samhain two months previously, helped assuage a particular source of imagined embarrassment for him - that of displaying his sexual prowess to the group. But, as the High Priestess had initiated him, sexually, into the coven, even his shyness of this particular taboo had faded into the ether. As she had first taken him within her arms, and then between her legs, and had encouraged him to explore and enjoy every inch of her fine middle-aged body, he had turned his eyes briefly to the rest of the coven and had found every last one of their number too lost in their own worlds of sexual congress to be wondering about his own intimate union.

Six women and five other men made up the membership of the coven, plus the High Priestess (who liked to be known as the Lady of the Land). All were people of high renown and none in their various communities could have even imagined such people embroiled in such a nefarious practice as Black Magic. To his immediate right stood the small and demure Mrs Canna - who was the village Post Office mistress. On the other side of her stood John Stuckey - a jocular magistrate from the nearby town. Also included in the coven was a local school headmistress, a professional artist, the owner of a large, nationally recognised garden centre, a lawyer - apparently of

117

some repute, a retired landlady, two councillors – both of Tory persuasion, and the owner of the local rag/newspaper. His good self and Angela, the detective from the local constabulary whom he had met at the hospital the previous Christmas and had since become intimately involved with, made up the final members of the coven, which was headed by The Lady of This Land. Despite questioning Angela, and doing some light research on the matter himself, he had learned little of the High Priestess' circumstances and believed her entire life to be made up by the workings of her coven.

There was no chance of any stray interlopers stumbling upon this unusual scene atop Solstice Hill. The neighbouring houses were now all owned by members of the coven, any of its stubborn previous owners having been made offers they could not refuse. To deter any random person from bumbling upon the coven's scandalous activities, a combination of razor wire, danger warnings and construction signs had been erected around the perimeter of the hill. Much of the warning signage and prohibitory fencing was made credible to outsiders by the new owner of Solstice Hill Farmhouse, the High Priestess herself, who had ordered much of the outer buildings and extensions of the farmstead to be demolished. This heavy work was necessitated to retrieve the ancient megaliths that had once formed the stone circle atop Solstice Hill and the place had been left looking like a building site for effect. The large stones had been hidden within the construction of the farmhouse extensions for their safety after receiving attacks by Christians at the height of that religion's hold on Britain. These stones had been returned to Soltice Hill and now formed the large megalithic circle the coven now stood within.

The Lady of the Land now stood before the roaring fire, her back to its frenzied, crackling flames. In her hands, held high to the sky, she held a long, thin golden sword. After a few incomprehensible words, the Lady of the Land called her circled coven to separate hands and step forward to warm their goose-pimpled flesh around the fire as she weaved her way through their number towards the outer circumference of the stone circle.

The doctor left the High Priestess to her devices, more concerned with warming his flesh and bones at the fire. He knew what she was doing anyway. With her sword, she was drawing a huge circle outside the perimeter of the stone circle. This would serve to protect the coven from whatever demonic force they dredged up from hell that night. This accomplished, the Lady and the Land would then draw a second circle - offering the coven double protection. To further defend them from attack, she would then inscribe three secret and powerful names of their God, whose identity, being a neophyte, he was still not yet privy to. The names inscribed were glyphs, almost runic in appearance. But they kept their mystery to those without the knowledge to interpret them wisely.

The High Priestess took her time with these ritual drawings - this even though the circles had been lightly pre-etched into the land earlier to ensure the accuracy of the symbols. When the two circles and the names inscribed between them had been completed, the doctor readied himself, knowing his part in the proceedings was nearing. As he made his way from the fire, the coven members he passed encouraged him by slapping his bare back enthusiastically or nodding earnestly at him. Miss Tasker, the school headmistress, even gave him a peck on his cheek, knowledgeable and appreciative of the role he was about to partake in the night's ritual.

The Lady of the Land was now on the outside of the circles and was completing her drawing of two squares in the ground, one within another - their points directed to the cardinal parts of a compass. At these corners, she inscribed further secret names, which the doctor hoped were aimed at his own personal protection.

The good doctor had joined this coven as a bit of a kink in his otherwise boring life. He had missed out on the sex and drugs other youths had enjoyed, having given his life completely to his study of medicine and gaining his doctorate. He had then married, but his need to commit to his role in the hospital was not a good recipe for a happy marriage and Elizabeth had left him, childless, within a couple of years of the Ceremony. And then he had me Angela, the Detective Chief Inspector, just the Christmas before, when the hospital beds had been filled with all kinds of strange medical incidents associated with this hill There had been something odd about that whole affair and his interest in the police investigations into those cases had fuelled his resultant relationship with the detective. Later, when their friendship and grown into a sexual relationship, she had explained to him the full history of Solstice Hill - not the bullshit of legends and hearsay, but the real power that could be harnessed from the site. She was involved in a powerful coven that had been convened to return the stone circle to the summit of Solstice Hill and to control and direct the power of the land there. Unbridled by the removal of the stone circle in previous years, the earth energies emitting from the hill had manifested in all sorts of dark and dangerous incidents, including those he had seen in the hospital the previous year. It was time, Angela had told him, to focus that energy. Then, as his life had become more involved and intertwined with that of the inspector, she had informed him that a place had become available in the coven. Not only that, she had persuaded the High Priestess for the good doctor himself to become an initiate in their circle. Intrigued and excited by the thought of orgies and a promised liturgy of unusually wild parties, he had readily agreed to join their number. They were, after all, a powerful group of people who could, perhaps, open doors for him that had remained stubbornly and stiflingly locked for him during the last few years. There was nothing to be afraid of, he had been assured.

Being a man of science, he had not been a true believer in all of his lover's talk of earth energies and witchcraft and magic. But his initiation ceremony into the coven, fuelled by all kinds of deliriants, had been one of the most exhilarating nights of his life. And he had to admit he had been excited in his anticipation of tonight's ceremony, despite Angela's concerns. But now, this particular ritual suddenly seemed a far more serious affair than he had bargained for. And for the first time, the doctor wondered just what, exactly, he had gotten himself into.

The frenzied flapping of wings brought him from his suddenly subdued thoughts. The High Priestess had now resumed her place within the circle, and the doctor felt suddenly abandoned, and more than a little uneasy. He looked across the naked bodies around the fire that now roared and crackled ferociously – as if it was fuelled from the depths of hell itself. Finally, he found Angela, but despite staring long and hard in her direction, her attention was centred on the High Priestess, who stood before the coven with the flapping chicken held high before her.

Held by its hind legs, the poor chicken flapped its wings frantically in the Lady of the Land's face as it struggled for its very life. In her right hand, the High Priestess grasped a smaller blade now, its sharp edge glinting red in the firelight. Then, in a single movement, she drew the blade across the chicken's throat. Hot blood trickled thickly over the bird's head and down over the Priestess' naked shoulders and breasts. The bird's wings continued to flap, even after the animal's death, spattering its draining blood across the priestess' face as well as parts of her body the thicker blood had missed. Instead of being sickened by the gory mess, the Lady of the Land seemed to relish the hot blood that covered her and her white teeth flashed crimson and she grinned through the bloody mask painted by her killing of an innocent life.

"With this animal's life, I conjure the almighty forces gathered here tonight to aid us in the resurrection of your power on Solstice Hill." The Lady of the Land pronounced loudly and clearly. "Give each one of us gathered here in this protected circle the power and strength to attain their wishes and deliver to them all that they command."

The doctor's eyesight blurred briefly and he rubbed at them to clear his vision. But his sight remained unfocused, more so now, and it wavered as though he watched the coven through a wall of intense heat. This was not an effect of the fire either, for looking down at his own naked, shivering body, that too now shimmered in and out of vision. The doctor remembered the drink he and the rest of the coven had shared before leaving the farmhouse and heading up to Solstice Hill for the ceremony. The drugs, apparently deliriants again, were now evidencing their power. He fell to his knees, his breath deepening as his heart grew faster and stronger.

The High Priestess spoke in Latin now, as far as the doctor could hear and decipher anyway. A few of the words reached him in full clarity, his understanding of the language from his school days, as well as his studies for his doctorate, letting him just about follow her words. "We welcome your return to this sacred land of old. Reward your servants of Solstice Hill this night with pleasures for our bodies and our minds.

And let us protect this land and use it to summon and maintain your presence amongst this earthly domain."

The coven started singing now - a different tune to the one they had employed during his initiation ceremony. Almost comically in his growing state of intoxication, he watched as the group began their excited orgy, all the while continuing their almost trance-like singing. The doctor felt lost, separated and abandoned from the proceedings. There was to be no physical pleasure for him that night.

Whilst the spectacle of the ongoing fire-lit orgy was certainly a scene to behold, the good doctor's strained eyesight allowed only the study of something closer to him now - a small white light that had suddenly appeared in the larger square before him. Confused by his mind drug-addled mind, and disorientated by his blurred vision, the light appeared to grow before him in both size and intensity. The orgy, a single fuzzy mass of swirling, undulating energy, appeared synchronised with the throbbing growth of the light in the outer square and it was then that the good doctor the light before him was a growing portal for the arrival of a demon conjured by the coven!

If only he could have avoided drinking from that poisoned chalice! But the High Priestess had handed him the drug-laced goblet personally to drink from and had stood before him as he had slurped down its contents. Christ, she had even looked into the emptied goblet once he had handed the damned thing back to her before filling it once more and moving on to the next member of the coven. It was almost as if she had suspected his motives for joining the coven.

The light now expanded until its brilliance physically filled the borders of the larger square about him and surrounded him in a wall of blazing light. It was then that its colour began to pulsate in a phantasmagorical light show. The good doctor was now imprisoned with the demon. And terrifyingly, the light, now almost a physical object in itself, now spilt over the edge of the demarcation line that edged the doctor's supposedly protected square.

Christ! Angela's caution towards tonight's ritual seemed to have been a prudent concern He had to forget the wild and abandoned sexual congress he had been hoping for this night. Now he knew for certain that he had been lured into the coven and that his square, not to make up the numbers but to be offered as a sacrifice!. He thought now of the documents he had been coerced into signing before he had been supposedly initiated into the coven. Like all the others in the group, by becoming a neophyte initiate into the coven, he had become part of their tight-knit family, and in doing so had signed away his entire worldly goods in a legally binding contract. Upon the death of any of the coven members, the entirety of their wealth would be shared out amongst its remaining numbers. He had, at the time of signing said documents, believed that as a slightly younger member of the coven, this would have served him to his advantage. He had believed that he would outlive at least a handful of the initiates and increase his own wealth in doing so. Some of the group were already of pensionable age, some by a good score of years. Back at the time when he signed that said contract, he had argued that when it was eventually his time to pass on, what care should he hold about who received his worldly goods? He had no children or even a family of his own. Of course, back then, he had thought that he would number amongst the coven membership for more than a few months. He felt cheated, outraged. And afraid.

To assuage her misgiving about tonight, Angela had read up on the ritual details she had gleaned about the mysterious proceeding ceremony. And she had made assurances to enact terrible and fitting revenge should tonight's event turn ugly for the good doctor. The detective inspector was, after all, a cunning woman indeed.

As the intensity of the imprisoning light about him increased to a degree where it now audibly rumbled, the doctor dug his bare hands into the earth beneath him. The soil was not as hard or crusted here as elsewhere on Solstice Hill that night as the wily inspector had secured certain precautions for his safety beneath the ground here She had watched the High Priestess earlier that day, secretly and from afar, of course. The Lady of the Land had visited Solstice Hill, as the detective knew she would, to lay out the geometrical guidelines of the sacred circle. As expected, she had included the addition of a square at the outside head of the circle. This was to safely contain any demon summoned within its boundary. As suspected, she had included the addition of a smaller square within the perimeters of the outer one. If they were to be effective, these outlines had to be inscribed with geometric perfection during the ceremony so, to save time in the dark and the cold and the dramatic theatre of the ritual, she had lain the groundwork of the protective symbols more carefully earlier in the day. All she then had to do on the night was to trace over the outline she had already carefully created on Solstice Hill.

As the High Priestess had finished her work earlier that day and had set off back to the farmhouse, Angela, knowing full well that it might be the good doctor who was destined as their sacrifice and not some tethered goat, had secreted within the ground contained in the smaller square a few items she had procured the year before - items taken at the time of her investigation into the strange events that took place at Solstice Hill the previous year, namely the bony hand a certain carpenter had hastily chopped from his own arm, a phial of blood taken from the teenage girl poisoned from the mushrooms picked from this site, and a small T-shirt acquired from the young boy who had murdered parents in the farm building the High Priestess had now made her home.

The doctor dug his raw bare fingers into the freezing earth beneath him. Retrieving the items from the ground, he threw them into the pulsating light, where they exploded into a display of colours he could hardly have imagined. The explosion of light suddenly spiralled around, away from the doctor, its massed confusion of colours passing over the square to circle, in an anti-clockwise motion, the large stone circle. Whatever demon lay amid the light had accepted its offering as acceptable and had now turned its attention to the coven itself, its power too great to be held by the High Priestess' square gaol. The growling demon now prowled the perimeter of the stone circle, whose boundaries had been built with far greater defences than those used in its original confining square.

As it tracked the Circle, Angela, having ruptured said protection with the sword the High Priestess had used to close the boundary, raced clockwise around the circle towards the doctor. As she reached him, she began constructing a protective circle around them both just before the demonic entity gained entrance into what immediately became an arena of bloodshed and suffering.

Inside the newly created circle, the doctor reached out and took Angela's hand. Both breathed heavily, their eyes open wide in horror and fascination as they listened to the screams and pains the rest of the coven suffered as they were torn apart. Their token embrace lasted only seconds, however as the demonic manifestation left the carnage contained within the circle and began rounding its outer circumference back towards her and the doctor.

Angela, separating herself from the doctor, stood proud, the tip of her sword pointing towards the approaching cacophony of light and sound. Angela held her ground as the ferocious source stopped outside the small magic circle. Keeping the point of her sword pointing at the demon she looked up into the starlit sky and took a deep contemplative breath. "Grant us the power we need to control all demons below your power. We have honoured you well, and have sacrificed our very coven to pay for our request. Master of this sacred land, give us the strength to keep Solstice Hill protected from outside interest and allow us to serve and revere this place. Let us be your aid in furthering your power in this world." The light, now shrunk to the size of a bear, now glowed like honey in the sunshine, its warmth more than welcoming in the shivering cold of the night. Angela turned to the doctor, lowering the ceremonial sword to her side. "It's alright." She said calmly. "It is friendly. It is pleased with our offerings tonight.."

The light shimmered and reduced in size until it presented itself as a ball of glistening gold light that hovered before them at head height. The drug-infused drink he had ingested earlier was taking full effect on the good doctor now and his abilities to distinguish reality from phantasm were confused and unreliable. "Fool." He shouted at Angela, still intensely fearful for his survival that night. He now turned on Angela, struggling to retrieve the golden sword from her hand to help protect them both from the demon. "He is the father of lies, remember?. He tricks your thoughts. Stay firm. Help protect us from this evil!"

The good doctor struggled to wrench the sword from his lover's hands.

Her strength felt insurmountable, however, as though her palms were glued to the golden dagger. And he soon gave up on his desire for control of the ceremonial weapon. Defeated, he stood deflated before Angela, breathless, his back to the looming power that grew once more.

"No. It is you who is the fool." Angela told him sternly. "All that has come to pass tonight has been planned. I have gained the power and wisdom of the whole coven now and will take sole ownership of this land. Unfortunately, the price for this power was high. I had to give up my coven. And, also, my lover."

"What are you talking about?" The doctor almost spat out his exclamation. But it was too late now for the good doctor and he instinctively knew it.

With a sense of theatre, Angela pushed the blade lightly at the doctor's chest, forcing the man to take a step backwards to avoid his flesh being punctured by its point. Suddenly pushed out of the protective circle, the good doctor stood naked and unarmed before the demon. Turning to address the threat, he did not even have time to voice his shock at Angela's betrayal before the glowing light exploded into a million dazzling unknowable colours...

... The good doctor found himself laying out in the open, still atop Solstice Hill. He sat up, grimacing at the early dawn light. The full moon hung low and heavy above the horizon, gently illuminating the blood-drenched stone megaliths before him with its pale silver light. At first, he thought he was alone – but he soon learned that was not really the truth - in two respects. First, in silhouette, though he recognised her figure immediately, despite now being clothed, he saw Angela as she made her way from outside the stone circle towards him. Standing over him, she held out her arms and pulled him to his feet, where she immediately knelt before him.

"It is done, my Master." She said, as she lay prostrate and in reverence on the icy floor before the good doctor.

He tried to speak but found his throat dry. And then he felt another, stronger voice rise from his throat. But before he heard what the voice said, he slipped away forever, into the chasm of darkness that was held within the shell of his body.

And that is the end of this particular tale. Together, we would now inherit Solstice Hill and all that it contained. And we would move into the farmhouse as an everyday couple. There,

133

we had a lot to put into action. We had much work to do, though I had no doubts that all we sought to achieve would now easily come to pass. After all, I had been calculating my plans for thousands and thousands of years.

Ushering Angela to stand, I nodded, accepting her obedience and worship. "Come," I said, motioning her to follow me. And I laughed, long and loud as I comprehended the full plethora of horrors I had planned for the world...

Chris Elphick

Thanks to Amber Seren Elphick for her story illustration for Gobble.

Printed in Great Britain
by Amazon